THE CANDIDATE

BY

JOSIE BROWN

PUBLISHED BY SIGNAL PRESS BOOKS

SAN FRANCISCO, CA

MAIL@SIGNALEDITORIAL.COM

Dear Dianna,
Hot Politics!
Enjoy!

DECEMBER 31ST

It was an unseasonably warm New Year's Eve, and the throbbing mass of partygoers centered around the fountain at the Bellagio was for the most part feeling no pain.

One in particular was especially numb. His captors had made sure of it, doping him up with a cocktail of drugs—a potent mix of zombie cucumber, scopolamine, and some botulism thrown in for good measure—that left him too paralyzed to move, to speak, to cry, let alone to shout out to the crowd that he was, quite literally, a ticking time bomb.

As the Bellagio's famous fountain pulsated to the sensual sounds of Sinatra, Carlos Rodriguez glared hard at those around him in the hope that someone—*anyone*—might be able to read the fear in his eyes, if not for his sake, then for the rest of them. Illuminated in the hotel's many roving spotlights, their faces melded into a living collage: flirting, blowing horns, laughing, and screaming. He tried to scream, too, but nothing came out. Not a whisper. The drugs ensured that.

Then there it was: *The countdown.*

58...57...56...

The last three months passed before his eyes, starting with the moment when that emotionless U.S. Customs official pulled him out of the employee line crawling down the gangplank of the Carnival Cruise ship on his one night of shore leave in Miami. If he had assumed that his Venezuelan passport wouldn't raise any flags with her, he was wrong. She asked him some seemingly innocuous questions about his purpose for coming into the country.

His answers, innocent enough, still landed him in some hot, dusty hellhole.

There, Carlos was stripped naked, shackled in a fetal position, or made to squat in his own waste. During the scalding heat of the day, he was given little water to quench his thirst, and no blanket when the night temperatures dropped to freezing. As bad as the daily beatings were, the threat of being drowned, tortured, or bitten by his captors' hounds of Hell was even worse.

He was no longer a man, only a number. They called him *Catorce*—the number, fourteen, in Spanish.

From the scared whispers and coded taps he heard from the other young *Venezueláños* also isolated in the prison's catacomb of cells, Carlos learned that, like him, they had all come from poor remote villages. None were married or had any immediate family, either back home or here in the United States.

In time, the *capitano* of their captors, the human devil named "Smith," told them that they were to play very important roles in the freedom and prosperity of both their old and new countries.

And that was how they were told that they were to be suicide bombers.

When that day—today—finally came, the men were taped down front and back with the bombs, then dressed in nice slacks, collared sweaters and beige cashmere jackets, their hair lightened and spiked. Yes, now they could easily pass as well-to-do gringos. Then they were drugged.

Two hours later, seven vans carrying the human bombs pulled up in front of the seven hotels hosting Las Vegas' world famous fireworks: the Flamingo, the MGM Grand, Circus Circus, Treasure Island, the Venetian and the Bellagio, all the way north to the

Stratosphere.

Only Carlos had been paired with another bomber: some kid, maybe seventeen or so, who had entered their hellhole only the day before. His captors called him *Trece*, the Spanish word for the number thirteen. Although muscle paralysis had set in quickly, Carlos's mind was still alert. He could tell that the boy, Trece, was also trying to fight the effects of the drugs. The look in his eyes wasn't terror, but determination.

Señor Smith had ridden shotgun in their van. When the van reached the Bellagio, Smith roughly yanked Carlos out the back. After positioning him in the heart of the teeming, screaming mass of humanity in front of the fountain, he slapped Carlos on his back and whispered in his ear: "Look at it this way—at least you and the others will die heroes' deaths for your new country..." before casually strolling away.

Out of the corner of his eye, Carlos watched as Smith reappeared with Trece the boy. They moved in the opposite direction though; deep into Bellagio's thickening crowd.

What had Smith called him, a hero? No, Carlos was more like a *fantasma*...

A ghost who would haunt the United States for years to come.

45...44...43...

At the thought of that, the tears that could not fall glistened in his eyes.

In front of him a cluster of unattached women unraveled quickly in order to sidle up to whatever single men were still around. Any moment now they would bestow the first kiss of the year on some lucky stranger, one of the joys of being young and single on this special night—

37...36...35...

One girl, pretty in pink, her blond hair grazing her bare

shoulders, glanced over at him. By her quizzical look he could tell she'd noticed his tears. She waved at him. Of course he couldn't wave back. No matter. Undeterred, she swam against the deep wave of humanity between them, to his side.

A burly red-haired man, watching the exchange, glared hard at Carlos. The fact that he didn't respond irritated the man, like a red flag waved at a moody bull. He grabbed the woman's arm, she tried to shake him off, but he shoved passed her, hell bent on reaching Carlos first.

Her boyfriend perhaps, determined to win her back? *Que lastima!* Perhaps the lovers could make amends in heaven, because in a mere twenty-two seconds, the bomb strapped to Carlos' chest would blow all of them to pieces...

DECEMBER 30TH, ONE YEAR EARLIER...

CHAPTER 1

"I hear you're one smooth sonofabitch."

Thanks to the hustle and flow of the Tilt'n Diner's dinnertime crowd, Republican Senator Andrew Jackson Mansfield's genial jibe was just loud enough to be heard by its intended party: Democratic political campaign strategist Ben Brinker.

Ben washed down a mouthful of the diner's whoopee cake pie with the last sip of his coffee and winked knowingly at his hosts—a couple of New Hampshire Democratic Party chairs—before facing his accuser. "Senator, if I've made you sit up and take notice, then I must be doing something right."

Unlike Mansfield's smile, Ben's was genuine, for good reason: at that moment his client, Congressman and recently declared presidential hopeful Richard Calder, was sharing his cozy vision of a Calder presidency with a reverential Katie Couric and all of America, including the New Hampshire voters gazing up at the television mounted over the diner's short order grill.

The flop sweat on the very young, very green campaign aide who was trailing Mansfield evidenced his relief that the senator's pique had been directed at Ben and not him. Ben, on the other hand, was used to being called all sorts of things by all sorts of people—especially those who, like Mansfield, were running for president, but didn't have a seasoned A-List sonofabitch of their own.

Specifically one who could get them an exclusive with Katie this early in the game.

To be honest about it, even Ben's clients were known to label him with a colorful name or two, particularly during a campaign. Smartass for sure. Bastard without a doubt. And yes, sonofabitch was a given. In Ben's mind that was all par for the course. Better he should piss off a client with a much needed reality check than watch him show his ass in public.

In any event, all was forgiven by the time the votes were tallied, because with Ben on your team *it was a given that you would win.*

Which is why the smart clients inevitably shut up, listened, and followed his advice.

And why, for the past twelve years, Beltway insiders had placed their bets on Brinker.

Even his dark horses were winners, and had been since his very first high profile campaign—for an incumbent senator whose unappreciated stance against his own party's policies put him some thirty points behind in the polls. But by election day, Ben had conjured up a slim but uncontestable lead by doing his usual voodoo: discerning the grittiest issues; crafting surefire sound bites that rallied those who might not otherwise go to the polls; and most importantly choosing an easy-on-the-eye candidate who appealed to female voters.

So when Ben jumped onboard Calder's presidential exploratory committee, bets on all the other Democratic candidates—both unannounced and already declared—were off. Hell, the kowtowing of these two state New Hampshire DNC party bigwigs between bites of the diner's celebrated White Mountain meatloaf was proof of that. Despite a field of six other party contenders, their initial polls of both declared Dems and independents were making Ben very happy. One had even slipped up and called the congressman "President Calder."

Hence, Andy Mansfield's crude albeit admiring declaration.

Yep, Ben Brinker was his party's consummate kingmaker, and everyone knew it. Why else had the dimpled Katie, gushing sweetness and light, put in the call herself yesterday, requesting that Calder grace her celebrated couch? Forget Diane, or Matt, or Anderson, or that constantly PMSing coven at *The View*. For his client, Ben had scored *the queen of daytime talk shows!*

As he shook Mansfield's hand, Ben couldn't help but size him up as a candidate. No doubt about it the senator had a lot going for him. The fact that he was six foot two, with a full head of hair and square-jawed good looks all certainly worked in his favor. It also helped that he hailed from North Carolina, a state coveted by both sides of the aisle for its swing electoral votes. Sons of the South rarely had problems garnering the votes of neighboring states, particularly if they were Republicans like Mansfield. He was a populist, but he had somehow skirted his party's Tea Party pressure cooker politics.

At forty-six years of age he would be the youngest candidate in the race. But in a presidential election, youth only reinforced any perceived inexperience. Granted, others had sidestepped that deficit: Clinton for one, not to mention Obama. Ben certainly knew how he'd make it a non issue for Mansfield: focus on his seven years as a senator, his middle-of-the-road voting history; his exemplary military record as a Marine fighter pilot with the renowned Checkerboards Squadron 312; and his seat on the Senate Arms Services Committee. And he'd have to make sure that the planks in his solidly populist platform were well-positioned with the media—

From Mansfield's gaze, Ben realized that the senator was also contemplating what might have been, if fate had played them different hands. And yet both men knew it was a moot exercise. In the first place, Ben worked exclusively with Democrats. Even if that weren't the case, from the looks of things the Republican powers-that-be were going to be backing Vice President Clemson Talbot, not some GOP upstart, no matter how ideal a candidate he might be.

Maybe that's why Mansfield is here without a real handler, thought Ben. He's lucky his wife—what's her name, Alice? Abigail?—has deep pockets. It's his only hope to hang in there.

Reality having set in, both men turned back to the TV just in time to see Richard Calder lose any chance of ever getting elected as Katie asked him, in a quiet but firm voice: "So tell me, Congressman, does the name Jenna McElvoy ring a bell?"

All the color drained out from under Calder's pancake makeup as she directed him to the monitor beside her. What materialized on it was Calder's long-time lover, a slight, pretty woman in her mid-thirties.

Fuck, no. Oh no, Ben thought.

Sitting beside Jenna was the love child she'd had with Calder: a cute four-year-old tyke named Cole. The boy was small for his age, listless and pale, even for television.

Then again, having a congenital heart disease will do that to a kid.

So yeah, Katie had contrived another perfect *gotcha!* moment. If there was any doubt to the contrary, she laid it to rest as she held up the next day's issue of the *Enquirer* and asked the congressman when, if ever, he planned on introducing Jenna to Sarah, his wife of thirty-one years.

"*Holy shit!*" Mansfield's aide hadn't realized that he'd uttered the oath out loud until he saw the doom in Ben's eyes. The kid stared down at his snow-spattered Florsheims.

In that nanosecond, Ben realized that his career had imploded along with his client's.

And if that wasn't enough of a tip-off, the strangled moans from the two New Hampshire Dem chairs said it all. They gathered their coats and scurried away from Ben without a backward glance. The snickers emanating from the Tilt'n Diner's counter regulars had them practically running out the door.

"Tough break, Brinker." Mansfield's sympathy seemed real. "I guess Calder's little extracurricular activity slipped by your vetting process."

Vetting process? Yeah sure, there was a time when Ben actually cared if his clients withstood a sniff test. But that was years ago, when he was still young and idealistic. It only took a campaign or two before Ben caught on to the fact that all politicians had skeletons in their closets. The goal was to keep them from popping out during the race. Why should one personal misguided indiscretion stop a good candidate's quest to improve the lives of all Americans?

He thought he had locked up Calder's good and tight—thanks to a $3,000-a-week cash withdrawal from a generous trust fund established by a cabal of Calder's closest good-ol'-boy supporters.

Obviously the *Enquirer's* offer had been somewhat more generous.

The smile Ben gave the senator this time was less cocky. "Yeah, well, pristine politicians are few and far between. If you know of one, give him my number."

Mansfield took out a business card and handed it to Ben. "Looks like you'll be having some free time on your hands. Headed back to D.C. tonight?"

Ben shrugged and nodded. No reason to stick around now.

"Great. Then why don't you stop by the Fairmont tomorrow evening, say, around eleven? The Colonnade Room. There's a little event being thrown, and I'm the guest of honor. Should give you a feel of what I'm about." With that the senator was gone.

Yeah, as if I'd ever work for a Republican, thought Ben. *Even I am not that desperate.*

He heard the buzz of his cell phone and pulled it out of his pocket. Chris Matthews' producer. He hit the mute button.

There was no good way to spin the Calder fiasco. But in good conscience, Ben couldn't yet turn in his resignation until Calder formally pulled out of the race. No doubt that would happen later that evening. Or even earlier, if Calder's wife had already gotten wind of the fiasco and was on her way down to the courthouse to file for divorce.

If he hurried, he could still make the last United non-stop back to D.C.

CHAPTER 2

"You sure are one stupid sonofabitch!" Congressman Calder's rant, roaring out of Ben's iPhone, could be heard by each and every wayward traveler in the Manchester Airport lounge, including the bartender who was trying hard not to smirk as he slid Ben's double Glenlivet, neat, in front of him. "Damn it, Brinker, you told me you had that bitch under control!"

Despite a splitting headache, Ben cradled his cell as close as he could to his head, then grabbed his glass as if it were a lifeline and took a swig. If he thought the scotch's numbing burn would muffle Dick Calder's profanity-laced bellowing, he was sorely mistaken. Worse yet, while Calder was screaming into one ear, Chris Matthews was barking his own ruminations about "the politician and his baby mama" on the lounge's TV set. His guest pundits—Paul Begala, Bay Buchanan, and Arianna Huffington, each wedged into a thin slice of the split screen—were spinning their own theories on the first scandal of the election season.

"Calm down, Dick! I did take care of her. I always do, don't I?" Ben ran his fingers through his hair. Three strands—all white—dropped on the bar beside his napkin. After today he wouldn't be shocked to find that they'd all turned white—or that they'd all fallen out. "I just talked to her yesterday in fact, and—Oh...wait!...*Shit!*"

"What now?"

"I—well...Okay, look: Last night I didn't have time to swing by there before my flight with—well, you know, her little stipend. I called instead, and told her I'd drop over tonight."

In all honesty, seeing Jenna never made Ben happy. He'd met her a decade ago, when she was one of the many fresh-faced bright young things on the Hill. Having just been hired on as a Staff Ass to her home state senator, she was a small-town girl with a sunny smile and great legs: something admired by Calder, among others—including Ben. And with so much going for her, Jenna wasn't exactly a saint. Then again, she wasn't a *Washingtonienne*, either. She truly believed Calder's bullshit when he told her he'd leave his wife for her.

At least, those first three or four years they were together.

Needless to say, when Jenna broke the news to him that she was pregnant, of course he hit the roof. Still, Jenna did her part. She left the Hill before her pregnancy could be discerned under her fitted suits.

Her discretion was part of her charm for Calder, whose wife gave him a wide berth but had made it ominously clear that the gates of hell would open up under him should any scandal threaten her hard-earned standing in Washington society.

As the executor of little Cole's trust, of course Ben knew otherwise.

Lately, though, Jenna had been fretting over what Calder's presidential aspirations would mean to her and Cole. She was no fool. Under normal circumstances she saw him, what, twice in a month? If Calder were to get the Democratic nomination, odds were he'd drop her like the hot political potato she was.

"And when he does, who's going to hire me? No one!" she'd fretted to Ben last night on the phone. "Not that Cole's illness isn't a full-time job. But without employment, I've got no health insurance. Ben, these medical bills are eating me alive, and that cheap son of a bitch Calder begrudges me every dime. I'm not living high on the hog here. I mean for God's sake, Cole is his son, too!"

No wonder Jenna had sounded so anxious on the phone last night. Besides whatever the Enquirer was paying, apparently she'd hoped to get her cash before the Couric interview aired.

Calder turned icy cold. "Let me get this right, Brinker: In other words, *you blew her off?*"

"No, not exactly. I mean—"

"Save it, Kiss Ass. For once, you may have done me a favor. At least I saved a few thousand there." Calder's cruel chortle sent chills up Ben's spine. "It'll be a cold day in hell when that cunt sees another buck from me. Her little gravy train is over. And so is yours, Brinker. It was your incompetence that lost me the election."

It was all Ben could do not to shout back into the phone, *You did this to yourself, shithead. If you'd loosened your wallet, she would have kept quiet forever.*

Instead he took a deep breath. "Can I help it that the *Enquirer* made her a better offer?"

His retort was met with silence. Then Calder hissed: "That's my point, you fucking moron. You should have come up with a more *permanent* solution. Like offing the bitch."

What the hell?

Yeah, okay. Lying to the media, to donors, even to his candidates' wives was one thing. And these days a payoff (to a dirty cop who could be convinced to "lose" an arrest warrant, or a blackmailer, let alone a loudmouth mistress) was just business as usual. But *arranging a hit?*

No, even *I* won't sink that low, thought Ben.

Ben knew the bartender had overheard Calder's taunt, too, because the stocky Irishman stopped polishing the counter mid-wipe and scrutinized him through hooded eyes. Ben pretended not to notice, but a moist trickle of shame inched its way down his back.

He turned his head in the hope of deflecting the man's stare. Then with as much dignity as he could muster, he muttered, "Seriously, Congressman, what do you take me for, some sort of thug?"

Calder cackled so hard that Ben had to hold the iPhone away from his ear. "A 'thug'? Frankly, that would be a step up for you, Brinker. Hell, a cockroach would be a promotion. For Christ's sake, you're just a fucking *political consultant*. Or have you forgotten that?"

If the cell hadn't chirped as the line went dead, Ben would have faked some sort of face-saving kiss-off for the benefit of the bartender and anyone else who was still listening, but why bother? Everyone was watching the television, anyway.

Ben's eyes gravitated there too when he realized what they were staring at: his photo, which had suddenly appeared on the television screen as Matthews spit out his name:

"—Is it just me, or has there been an epidemic of political scandals lately? Seems like the only thing they have in common is the same political consultant: Ben Brinker. Remember the congressman from Utah who was caught last month soliciting teenage girls over the Internet?"

The screen cut back to the pundits. "Well, yeah, that was Ben's candidate, too." Begala's nod was accompanied with a grimace. "But hey, Chris, we political consultants don't carry crystal balls. And the 'Mr. Smith Goes to Washington' types are few and far between—"

"If I remember correctly, Brinker also handled that governor who recently got indicted in a construction kickback scandal." Bay shook her head in disgust. "And didn't he work on the campaign of that senator whose diplomatic aspirations went up in smoke faster than you could say 'back taxes'? Whitewashing the depraved makes you just as culpable, in my book."

"Granted, there are some pathetic losers up on the Hill, but there are also some really great statesmen—*and* stateswomen." Chris was just warming up. "They just don't hire creeps like Brinker."

"Bottom line is that Brinker's the best at putting lipstick on pigs and running them for office." Arianna's icy chuckle pierced right through Ben. "But seriously, how many political consultants can survive in D.C. with those kind of 'see-no-evil, hear-no-evil' antics? It may work if you're a candidate's wife, but not a campaign strategist who wants to stay on K Street."

Damn, that's harsh, hon. Well then hell, don't count on me blogging anytime on HuffPo...Yeah, okay, so it's a long shot that, after this Calder crap, you'll ever ask me again.

"Nah, something else is going on here!" Matthews was on a roll. "Maybe some lousy karma. 'Bad Luck Brinker' is some sort of political cooler who jinxes his candidates' chances—"

This set off a cacophony of supposition, innuendo and balls-to-the-wall blarney from his guests. Above it all Matthews roared his patented, *"Tell me something I don't know!* Be right back—"

All eyes in the bar turned to Ben.

Hit with the realization that his income stream had just dried up—worse yet, that he wouldn't be able to replace it because he'd never live down this latest humiliation—the Tilt'n Diner's signature whoopee cake pie crawled back up Ben's throat, along with his Glenlivet neat.

Swallowing hard, he tossed a ten on the bar and, with what dignity he could muster, walked to the men's room.

Once inside, he kicked open an empty stall, and promptly threw up.

"I never thought I'd ever hear from you again." It was Jenna's idea that they meet far out of town, and suggested Brookside Gardens, in Silver Spring. Ben could see why. Ever since the Couric interview, the media had been hounding her like a pack of wolves. At this frigid time of year, the gardens would be empty.

Of course, the last thing he needed was any further association with Calder, or with Jenna either, for that matter. But no; he had to do this one last thing.

Ben hardly recognized her. Not only was she thinner and more haggard but for once she didn't have Cole at her side. "Where's the little guy?"

"With his physical therapist, so I don't have much time." Jenna's eyes darted constantly as she scanned the empty rows of bushes, as if someone might be lurking. He couldn't blame her for being antsy. Still, knowing her, he had no doubt that she was too ashamed to look him in the eye. "So what do you want, Ben?"

"Here. Take this." He opened the bag he was carrying and pulled out a book: *David Copperfield.*

She stared down at it, puzzled. "Is this for Cole?"

"Yeah, you could say that. There's a hundred dollar bill at the beginning of every other chapter. It's not much, but still. I know you can use it."

Tears glazed her soft brown eyes. "But—I thought, after last night...He wants me to have it anyway?"

Ben shrugged. "We both know Dick better than that."

"Jeez, Ben, he'll hit the roof when he finds out you did this." The hand she laid on top of his was the one with which she'd wiped away her tears. The dampness comforted him.

"I don't give a flying fuck. And neither should you. Besides, the way I had the account set up, there's nothing he can do about it." He sighed. "Not that it matters now, but just out of curiosity, how much did you get for the interview anyway? It better have been worth it."

"A quarter of a million."

Ben winced. "Damn, Jenna. There was eight times that amount in Cole's account. Between the two of us we'd have convinced him to raise your allowance."

"Like you said—we both know Dick better than that."

"But you know me, too. Jenna. Do you think I could have done that to you? To Cole?"

Her lip trembled, but she held her head steady. "Not in a million years—once upon a time. But I couldn't risk finding out the hard way you weren't that guy anymore." She hugged the book to her chest. "I'm sorry, Ben. Forgive me."

"Nothing to forgive." Because he knew she was right. In this town you were judged by the company you kept.

And right now Ben had no friends.

Then he remembered Andrew Mansfield's offer.

JOSIE BROWN

CHAPTER 3

"If Mansfield offers you a job, you'd be a fool to turn it down."

Supreme Court Justice Roberta Gordon was knee deep in manure—literally—and loving it. Mulching her organic garden with the stuff was her favorite way to pass a blustery winter weekend.

And because Ben would always appreciate everything she'd done for him, he hung in there with her, even though the stench was nearly intolerable.

While a college freshman at Berkeley, he had worked on Roberta's first campaign for California state attorney general. By her third term in that position, he was advising her re-election bid, along with the campaigns of a half-dozen other politicians in the state. It was during that term that she had been nominated for a seat on the U.S. Supreme Court.

In time Ben's own successes also brought him to Washington. Many of the candidates he'd worked for had heard about him from Roberta, who sang Ben's praises to anyone who asked.

His loyalty to her was just as steadfast. In fact, she was the only politician he'd ever truly come to trust.

Sadly, she was also the only woman who'd earned his trust. Which was why he'd asked her, on numerous occasions, to just name the day and he'd marry her.

Without fail, she'd blush at the thought, then mutter, "Why

Benjamin Brinker, I'm old enough to be your mother! Besides, if I wanted my very own boy toy, I'd certainly choose someone a bit younger—although your upper body definition isn't bad for someone of your age. That said, you've only yourself to blame if you can't find a woman who'll put up with you."

Today though, instead of debating their chances of marital bliss, she kept him focused on a topic he refused to take seriously: why he should take Andy Mansfield up on his offer to run his campaign.

He knew she meant business when she dumped a wheelbarrow of cow dung onto the rosebushes then clapped her hands to indicate that it was his duty to spread it around. "Seriously, Ben, when did you give up believing that candidates should stand for something? Otherwise you're no better than a K Streeter, or a beltway bandit."

"Ouch, Roberta! That's cruel."

"The truth hurts more than a smack upside the head. Although lately I've been tempted to give you the latter." Her smile faded. "You couldn't do any better than Andy Mansfield. And let's face it: he certainly votes with more care than a lot of our clan."

"Yeah, yeah, I know." Gingerly he patted the manure around a bush tagged Pink Double Knock Out. If she insisted on these hands-on tête-à-têtes, the very least she could do was provide a facemask. As it was, the only thing that saved him from heaving his Five Guys burger into the dung heap were the thick gloves she'd tossed his way. He smiled slyly. "Why are you so enthralled with this guy, anyway? You can break it to me gently: Should I be jealous?"

"Ha! You just wish someone would sweep me off my feet so you'd be off the hook." Dusting the dirt from her sleeves, she stood up and surveyed his handiwork. The glint in her eye told him he could now plop down on one of the two sun-bleached Adirondacks and pour himself a hot toddy from the thermos on the side table. "Besides, Mansfield is head over heels in love with that sweet Vandergalen heiress he married, so that will never happen."

At least with Mansfield I won't have to worry about bimbo eruptions, thought Ben.

"I'll bet you didn't know that he's the only member of this Congress who has ever argued a case in front of the Supreme Court, and won." Roberta took a satisfying sip.

"Ha. No wonder you're so high on the dude."

"Darn tootin' I'm high on him. During his summation, he was succinct, reverential, and quite persuasive. He even had our esteemed chief justice eating out of his hand." She shook her head, marveling. "It was about two years before he was elected senator. The case revolved around a convicted alien's rights: some guy from Venezuela who'd had the misfortune to get arrested driving a stolen car. Turned out the car had been stolen by his employer, but they were going to deport the Venezuelan anyway. The suit was filed against the U.S. Attorney General's office."

"Interesting that the client was Venezuelan. That was right before Padilla toppled Chávez's handpicked goon, wasn't it? I would have guessed that a boy scout like Mansfield wouldn't have taken it on. Considering Talbot needs his own Axis of Evil, Venezuela gives our creepy veep a great place to start. He's made it his mission to crucify anyone Venezuelan—that is, until his puppet dictator was in place."

"That's why you two would make such a great team. I'm just being selfish." Roberta pulled off her gloves. "Ben, I have something to tell you, in the strictest confidence. I'm leaving the bench. I'm turning in my resignation on New Year's Eve."

Ben dropped the manure with a thud. "But you love the court! You were meant to be there, Roberta. The way it stands now, you're its moral compass."

Roberta laughed. "That is certainly kind of you to say. But

sadly, the doctors give Mother just six months to live. She raised me on her own, Benjamin. We didn't have a pot to piss in, but she worked day and night so that I could finish college, and then continue on to law school. This is the least I can do for her. All the more reason I should leave now, while Barksdale is still president. Should the vice president take his place..."

She was too upset to finish the sentence.

She didn't have to. He knew what she meant.

It was why she was pushing so hard for Mansfield.

Roberta stood directly in front of the December sun. It radiated around her like a halo.

How appropriate, he thought. She's an archangel seeking justice for all mankind.

"Why not help elect a man who follows his own convictions? Maybe he'll rub off on you a little. Remember, Benjamin, in the final analysis it's not the party; it's the candidate and his platform. Consider it your shot at redemption." She pointed to the manure. "Now, no more lollygagging! It's time to mulch the hydrangeas."

————————

Venezuela's Padilla Nationalizes USCo Oil
After Failed Takeover

12/31 - CARACAS (Reuters) – Venezuela's president, Manolo Padilla, announced today that he has nationalized USCo Oil Corporation's multibillion-dollar investments in the country's massive Orinoco reserve.

Whereas four other oil companies have agreed to negotiate deals involving current and future participation in projects based in Venezuela, USCo, the United States' largest oil producer, refused to sign an accord that, in effect, would have transferred operations of the six heavy crude upgrading projects to Padilla's Ministry of Petroleum.

The Venezuelan president also ruled out paying cash compensation, or buying the debt they took on to develop the projects.

———————

CHAPTER 4

It was Vice President Talbot's idea, and Smith had to admit, it was sheer genius: Whenever the two men had the need to talk, the vice president gave Carl, his usual Secret Service driver, the day off. Then he had his assistant, Eloise, call in Mr. Smith as Carl's substitute. Having once been in the Service (Presidential Protection Detail, in fact) and the Agency, Smith already had all the necessary security clearances.

There, in the privacy of Talbot's armored limo, the two discussed anything they wanted. On that crisp, frigid first morning of the New Year, the topic at hand was the undoing of a government.

Specifically, that of Venezuela's dictator, Manolo Padilla.

Since Padilla's ousting of USCo Petroleum that morning, Mr. Smith had been anticipating the vice president's call. That Talbot had waited until that evening had demonstrated unusual restraint on his part.

"Already the old men are on the warpath! Do you know how much of a financial loss this means? And trust me, it's not just the USCo holdings that are at stake here." Talbot's breathing was labored. Whenever he was upset, like now, he paused between words.

What a sniveling pussy, Smith thought, but he kept his mouth shut and let the other man rant. The limo, flanked front, back and on both sides by the usual battalion of black SUVs loaded down with Talbot's Secret Service detail, was supposed to be on its way to the White House, where he was to join Mrs. Talbot, who was already with the president and his family, ringing in the New Year. But at Talbot's behest, Smith went by way of the National Mall. Talbot's favorite monument was the Lincoln Memorial. It gave Smith a chuckle to think of the vice president attempting to channel Honest Abe.

"That bastard Padilla has started the process of cutting us off from our oil supply! The Chinese are filling the void in purchasing it quite handily. He's taking all those yuans and buying guns from those Russian whores, as if it's World War III already! And considering how the rest of South America feels about his oil—and about us—he won't have any problem carrying out that little fantasy." Talbot leaned forward and lowered his voice to a hiss. "And if he does, Smith, it's all your fault. If I remember correctly, when we liberated Venezuela from Maduro, it was you who suggested that we lend him our support, and all that implies."

Smith blinked, but said nothing. He'd anticipated that accusation since the moment Talbot had squeezed his stocky girth into the backseat of the limo. Someone else was always the fall guy, right? Well, unfortunately for Talbot, Smith wasn't going to fall on his sword, let alone put a bullet behind his own ear. And Talbot knew better than to sell him out.

If he ever tried, Smith had a few insurance policies to cover that scenario.

"Something's got to be done about it immediately." Talbot leaned back with a grunt. "In fact, the timing couldn't be better, now that the mid-terms are over."

"We'll never be able to take him out in some covert op. He knows us too well."

"You're disappointing me." Talbot met Smith's eyes in the rearview mirror.

"I don't mean to. I'm just leveling with you. It will take something different this time."

"What are you suggesting?"

"If the incident that precludes our takeover were to happen here, on American soil—"

Talbot cringed. "What, are you nuts?"

"Hear me out: A 'terrorist act' with Padilla's fingerprints all over it will ensure that our invasion of Venezuela has the full blessing of the American people, the Congress, and the world." He turned to face Talbot. "And if you're the squeaky wheel warning about it throughout the election cycle—"

"No! Too devastating...Should anyone find out—besides, the old men wouldn't like it, either."

Smith shrugged. "I'm just saying it's a slam dunk."

"Too bad. It's off the table." Talbot shifted his bulk so that he could stare at the frigid wonderland beyond the limo's back window. "Look, everyone has an Achilles' heel. We both know that. Padilla's is what, women? Gambling? Drugs?"

Smith knew Talbot was right. But he also knew not to let the vice president in on that, or he wouldn't get what he wanted from him. "His private physician may be our way in. Particularly with the right incentive."

"And what would that be?"

"Blackmail. The kidnapping of a family member. This isn't brain surgery. Although, if we make the right threat, it might be the way to take Padilla out: some kind of fatal surgical procedure, the wrong meds, perhaps an overdose. Damn that socialized medicine, eh?"

As he hoped, that brought out a belly laugh from Talbot. "No shit. Okay, sounds like a plan. Go for it." His smile dissolved. "Now, about the election: Anything interesting I should know about?"

Smith thought for moment. "We've got rats burrowed deep within each of the candidates' campaign headquarters. As usual, the Dems are scrounging for dirt on each other. While they do all the heavy lifting, we just lean back and take notes."

Talbot chuckled. "Great. It should be interesting to see who's the last man—or woman—standing when all is said and done. Then we use the intel to shred the rep of whoever it is. It's an equal opportunity massacre. You've got to love this country. "

As casually as he could, Smith adjusted the rearview mirror, but really he was double-checking that the digital audio bug he'd hidden there upon entering the vehicle was receiving loud and clear. He'd remove it when he left the vehicle, before Talbot's PPD did its next bug sweep.

Yessiree, Smith was a firm believer in personal insurance policies.

CHAPTER 5

The care and feeding of Andrew Mansfield's most generous campaign donors was well underway by the time Ben got to the Fairmont on that drizzly New Year's Eve. Dinner was served promptly, the Tattingers flowed freely, and the up-tempo tunes emanating from the ten-piece orchestra on the Colonnade Room's center stage lured a constant wave of the senator's well-heeled guests onto the dance floor, so few if any of them minded the long wait to be endured prior to partaking in their prime objective: a few fleeting but memorable moments with Mansfield, in which he shook their hands and intoned a heartfelt thanks to them for ponying up $2,500-per-person for a plate of the Fairmont's renowned Shenandoah Valley grilled rib eye of bison, the proceeds of which would go to the Mansfield Presidential Exploratory Committee fund.

As requested, Ben, tuxedoed and manure-free, arrived punctually at eleven o'clock. Waiting for him at the ballroom's double-door entry was Sukie Carmichael, Mansfield's aide-de-camp, a slight spinsterish woman with an unruly red mane. He followed her lead as she wove around banquet tables and partying revelers.

They ended up in front of a door that was hidden behind a few potted ferns. In the small anteroom on the other side of it were two men. Immediately Ben recognized the eldest as Preston Alcott III—the managing partner at Cochran Adams Webster and Alcott, the oldest, most revered law firm in Washington. Besides being a celebrated lawyer, Alcott served as gatekeeper to the country's aristocracy. The sway he held over statesmen, monarchs, even dictators the world over was legendary.

The esteemed attorney was in his mid-seventies but could easily pass for a much younger man—ramrod straight and broad shouldered as he was. Even seated, Ben could tell he was a tall man. His eyes were piercingly bright, and befitting his role of patrician, his hair was full and white.

Ben had done his research. He knew that Alcott was also the executor of Abigail Vandergalen Mansfield's trust, not to mention the blind trusts of the current POTUS and his wife, Edward and Sarah Barksdale, and the estates of an impressive percentage of the Forbes 400. No doubt Alcott was there to ensure that Abby's very expensive investment in her husband's political career would pay off in the largest and most important dividend of all: executive power.

Alcott's presence there was proof that Ben wouldn't be handed the job carte blanche.

Fuck it. I need to score this gig—and a win—to prove I'm back in the game, even if that means kissing Alcott's ass, thought Ben. So it's show time.

As Sukie made the introductions all around, Ben shook Alcott's hand and gave a reverential bow. "It's an honor, Mr. Alcott."

"Ah, the kingmaker," Alcott declared.

Ben held his cursory gaze. "No sir. That would be your title, not mine."

Alcott's slight nod indicated his grudging approval at the response, but Ben was fully aware that the real grilling hadn't even started.

The man standing with Alcott chuckled nervously. Still his handshake, two-handed and firm, made up for his obvious apprehension in the presence of Alcott. "Paul Twist. I'm Andy's finance chair."

Ben recognized the name. "Also a partner at Cochran Adams. And Andy's best friend. You guys roomed together in law school, right? It's a pleasure to meet you, too."

Andy's buddy's nodded genially. "Your track record is a thing of wonder, Mr. Brinker. But you've yet to manage a presidential campaign, am I right?"

"Yes. In that regard, the senator and I are both underdogs going into this thing." *What, did you think I wasn't going to point out that your boy doesn't have his own party's blessing? Fat chance.* "We both know the deciding factors differ every four years. But one thing doesn't change: The candidate who wins is the one who has the ability to embody the message the public wants to hear, to get that message out to the media, and to respond immediately to any bullshit that the other side might toss our way. As my track record shows, it's what I bring to the table."

"That's all well and good. It's too bad it didn't work for Calder." Alcott's smile said it all: You lose.

Upon hearing the congressman's name, Ben gave an involuntary wince. "As long as you can assure me that Senator Mansfield's, er, *skeletons* aren't anywhere near as fertile, I'll take your candidate all the way to the White House—"

Andy Mansfield's hearty laugh roared through the anteroom. Ben looked up to find the senator standing in the doorway. He had his arm around a woman of slight build and medium height, with long pale hair pulled back severely from her anxious face and twisted into a chignon. Ben recognized her immediately: Abigail Vandergalen. She was, perhaps, eight years younger than her husband. Her black gown, a sequined sheath that she wore under a cropped lace jacket, was obviously expensive, but its elegance was undermined by the slump of her shoulders and her pensive grimace. Her squared-off pumps didn't help, either.

In fact, if Ben had to choose one thing that stood out about Abigail Vandergalen Mansfield, he'd say not a thing—

Except for her eyes, which were deep set, and as blue and sparkling as rough-cut sapphires—at least, from what he could tell in the few seconds in which they actually met his, before her innate shyness forced her to turn away again.

Unfortunately her small thick-framed glasses did nothing to enhance them. *Damn shame she has so little charisma. We'll have to get her into media training yesterday to keep that from hurting Mansfield on the campaign trail—*

Andy nodded at all three men, but it was Ben whom he slapped on the back. "These two will swear up one side and down the other that I'm holier than a saint."

"And they should know, I presume."

"There is only one person who knows me better. I'd like to introduce you to Abby."

Ben gave her his patented thousand-watt smile. "Pleased to meet you, Mrs. Mansfield."

"Call me Abby, please. And I hope you'll allow me to call you Ben." This time when she looked up at him, her eyes didn't waver. In fact they seemed to look right through him. "You'll have to excuse us for being tardy, Mr. Brinker. I was still on the dance floor when you arrived."

"And giving an earful to some very earnest young man from the Auto Alliance. He was naive enough to insist that Detroit is doing all it can to cut emissions." Andy gave his wife's arm a squeeze. "You see, my wife has made the reduction of our country's petroleum consumption her personal mission."

"To the point where she insisted that I divest her portfolio of any and all oil company stocks, and buy into clean energy start-ups instead." Alcott's disapproval was evidenced by the disdain in his voice. "One's personal ideology shouldn't impinge on one's investment strategy."

"I've always appreciated your concern over my financial matters, Preston. You know that." Abby's tone was soft, but firm. "But I refuse to support industries that are the problem, not the solution. Don't you agree, Mr. Brinker?"

"Personally, my philosophy is 'whatever floats your boat.' Heck, I know people who choose their stocks the way others pick horses at the racetrack: because they like the name. It's all a game of chance, right?" He shrugged. "Now if you're asking my professional opinion, I'd say your instincts—be those personal or political—are ingenious. In fact, if a list of your green investments were to be 'accidentally' leaked to a few of the right reporters, they'd be duly impressed that you put your money where your mouth is. And what they'd write would sway a lot of independents and undecideds, not to mention any Dems looking to come our way."

"But we don't just 'dabble in stocks.' For the past six years in a row, my husband has been voted the greenest Republican in the Senate. We're making inroads in convincing our party that being green isn't just environmentally smart—it's also fiscally responsible. Some of the country's greenest business visionaries have stepped up and offered their support. They're excited that Andy is making the greening of America a national mandate. If we're going to—well, to put it somewhat indelicately, quit sucking on the 'tit' of foreign oil—we have to stop cold turkey."

Ben nodded, impressed. "You're right, Abby. That message coming from a Republican candidate is big news."

Andy smiled. "You now see, Brinker, why I've come to realize that Abby's instincts are always right on the mark. In fact, it's why you're here tonight."

"How so?"

"It was Abby who suggested that I approach you to run my campaign in the first place."

Abby turned away shyly. Andy, on the other hand, smiled at

Ben's obvious disbelief. "Even before we ran into each other, she said—and she's correct—that crossing Talbot would be political suicide for any of our party's favored campaign advisers, so we should find the best Democratic consultant; someone who knows how that party thinks—and how to strategize against our frontrunner. And someone who wouldn't be afraid to take the gloves off, when the time came. As always, she called it. So I guess Calder's implosion was my good fortune. And yours." He gave Ben a knowing grin. "Which is why I'm hoping you've passed Preston's inquisition."

"Times will be a lot tougher, Andrew, if this boondoggle of yours doesn't pay off." Alcott took a sip of his drink. "Six hundred million is a lot of money to bet on a long shot. And if you lose, so does Abby, since it's her money that will be the initial seed capital for your campaign. As you can imagine, the thought of that makes me very uncomfortable."

"But he won't lose." By the way Abby said it Ben could tell that she wasn't being naive, but just stating the facts as she saw them. "Certainly Vice President Talbot has his supporters. In the past, they've funded him fully—and have prospered, along with him, based on a failing energy policy. However the rest of us are ready for new leadership, both in the party and in the White House. With your help, Ben, that will be Andy."

So the mouse isn't afraid to roar. Interesting.

"As you can see, Preston, Abby is one hundred percent behind backing my campaign—and behind Ben, too. And as always, she has the last word." Andy's point was made: Game over.

At that, Alcott gave a resigned shrug. Paul, on the other hand, tried to hide his smirk.

Knowing he'd trumped any argument to the contrary, Andy turned to Ben. "So what do you say? Are you in?"

Hmmm, thought Ben, Now let me get this straight: I get to redeem myself with a candidate who is a seasoned politician from a large swing state, and whose wife has a trust fund that rivals Iceland's gross domestic product. To top it off, he's as pure as driven snow...

Hell yeah, where else would I be?

Not that he had to say that out loud. His smile said it all.

Andy shook his hand. "Great! You'll make a great wingman. We have a few minutes before I jump onstage to ring in the New Year. Let's compare notes on New Hampshire —"

CHAPTER 6

She was nicely naughty, a raven-haired sylph with a sleek chin-length bob and a come-hither beauty mark on the left side of her luscious lips. One dainty foot, encased in a high-heeled diamond studded ruby slipper, was propped high on the rung of the bar stool next to her, unleashing her leg—long, strong, lean, and slim at the ankle—from the skin-tight red velvet gown sliced high on her thigh.

There was nothing Ben wanted more than to play her Prince Charming.

Hell, why not? It was just a few minutes before midnight. His timing was perfect.

He had zoned out somewhere in the middle of Andy's speech. There were only so many ways a politician can inspire his constituency, and Ben had heard them all before. In a long career he would hear them all again.

So instead he searched out the nearest bar. Time to celebrate his resurrection.

There was one in the back of the ballroom, but the line was too long. But the second one, in the hotel lobby right outside the ballroom's open door, was empty—

Except for Little Red Ride Me Hard.

Of course at that point he just *presumed* she'd live up to that fantasy. Still, he'd be willing to bet on it. The giveaway was what he saw on the spot where her backless gown came to a vee at the base of her spine:

A tattoo of a broken heart.

Perfect. He liked his women heartbroken. That keeps it simple. She wouldn't expect it to go beyond tonight.

Particularly on New Year's Eve, when no one wants to go home alone.

He wondered if he'd still be able to make out his candidate's punch lines from the barstool beside Red Velvet. The senator's jokes seemed to be going over big with the crowd, if the waves of laughter emanating from the room were any indication.

Yeah, no problem, he thought. Mansfield was coming in loud and clear...

If Ben cared to listen at all.

A sleek blade of her hair sliced her milky shoulders as she threw back her head and nudged a last lethargic drop from her martini glass.

"The lady will have another. And a scotch, neat, for me." He skirted a twenty toward the bartender.

"Do I look that easy?" Red Velvet pretended to pout but couldn't hold it together. Her full-throated laugh was an outright dare.

Easy? Heck, yeah.

And for some reason, she looked familiar, too. Something about the slant of her cheek. Or maybe he had once lost himself in the deep mossy depths of those luminous eyes peeking out under those brow-grazing bangs...

No, if he had met Red Velvet before, he would have certainly remembered. He shook his head. "If you want my opinion, I'd say you look thirsty." He slid onto the bar chair next to her. "Besides, who wants to drink alone on New Year's Eve?"

"Who says I'm alone?"

Ben made the grand gesture of craning his neck around her then shrugged. "Unless you're dating the Invisible Man, I'm your best bet."

This time her smile was a bit forced. "Yeah, that's my guy. *Invisible.* But you'll still have to convince me that you're the better man."

"Don't doubt that I can."

"I won't. Not in a million years—" she murmured, drinking him in. As she casually took the object of his affection—that beautiful leg—and crossed it over its perfect match, he felt his cock harden—"but you'll have to try hard, just the same."

That was when he kissed her.

It stunned her. He could tell by the tiny gasp she gave. He barely heard it though, because just then the crowd began the countdown to midnight—

58...57...56...

He could hear Mansfield's voice booming above it all: "Ah, here we go! And wouldn't you know it, I've lost my wife! Abigail? Abby? Come on up here, honey, don't be shy—"

That was when Red Velvet dream bit his lip then licked the wound so lovingly, so passionately.

For a moment there, he almost forgot to breathe.

CHAPTER 7

She held onto him, and didn't let go.

Not as they walked down the hall, or even as they rode the elevator down to the hotel's garage. It was all he could do not to take her right then and there, grab hold of the slit in her dress and rip it all the way up. Instead, he gritted his teeth and held himself back...

But only until they got to his place.

It tore with ease. And as great as she looked in red velvet, she looked so much better out of it. Even when freed by the gown's boned bodice, her breasts¬–plump, their nipples large and erect–rode high over her taut abdomen, her narrow shoulders creating an illusion that they were even more generous.

Her moans drove him crazy. Or was it the way she teased his large, stiff cock with her fingers until he felt he would burst? He couldn't tell...

Then again, did it really matter?

No, of course not. All that counted was that her sweet musky smell was beckoning him, letting him know that she was wet and waiting for him. He plunged deep inside of her, ignoring her as she cried out in pleasure.

They were a tight fit, but he could tell she loved it too, by the way she immediately matched his rhythm, stroke by stroke. He tried to hold back as long as he could, God help him, but she shuddered as she came, and he couldn't help but erupt.

Then they laid there, their bodies tangled, soiled, sopping in sweat...

But not for long.

"My turn," she gasped, panting, into his ear.

Her eyes, deep jade pools, challenged him to explore every inch of her. Slowly, gently, he kissed the tiny mole over her left breast. Then he flipped her over so that he could admire her high firm ass, kiss that broken heart tattoo.

That's when he noticed some odd scars, a few burns, on her legs and her arms.

"The Invisible Man left his mark, eh?" Suddenly, he felt a tightness in his chest.

"Calm down, Sir Lancelot. No one went at me with a lit cigar." She arched her back tauntingly. "I'm a sculptor. When you hack away at metal, there are lots of opportunity for cuts and blowtorch burns."

He could breathe again. "A sculptor? Well then, you should be honored to know you're my first." He stroked her slowly between her legs, enjoying how she shivered at his touch. "And I assume I'm your first political consultant."

"Is that what you are?" She laughed so hard that she almost rolled off the bed. Then, to steady herself, she took his fingers to her lips and kissed them. "Don't tell me you work for Mansfield?"

"Well, yeah, as a matter of fact. As of last night."

"Ha." She shrugged. "From the looks of that adoring crowd, would you say he needs much help?"

"All candidates have their acolytes. But if he's going to knock Talbot out of the game, he'll need a lot more of them. Believe me, it won't be easy." Nor was it easy for Ben to keep focused on their conversation.

Not with her on top of him now, stroking him back to life.

"You and I both know that these revival meetings are just for show," she murmured between gasps. "His wife has enough money to pay off his election expenses without batting an eye. Andy Mansfield is the *last* guy who's going to go hat in hand to the Feds for matching funds. But he's still got to impress the old man, Alcott. That's truly the *only* way to knock Clemson out of the box—"

As hard as it was for Ben to do so, he pulled her off of him. "You know a hell of a lot, for a sculptor—"

"I read: WaPo, Daily Kos, HuffPo, Politico, Andrew Sullivan. Hey, can I help it if I'm a political junkie?" She stroked his nipple, and placed his hand on her breast so that he'd take the hint that he could certainly do the same to her.

"A junkie, or a groupie?" The thought of having his very own groupie made him hard again—but then he drooped at the thought that she'd be just as willing to jump in the sack with any of his Dem competitors, too.

Or, God forbid, a Republican adviser. Since Ben had met her at a GOP candidate's fundraiser, that was certainly possible—

A fundraiser for the handsome, charismatic Andrew Mansfield.

"So, have you met Mansfield?" He tried to keep his voice casual, but it cracked anyway.

If she noticed, she didn't show it. "Of course. But I know his wife better. So, yeah, he's got my vote." She nuzzled Ben's ear. "If you're asking, I can honestly tell you that you're my very first political consultant. And certainly my last."

"Why? Was it that painful for you? Didn't I do justice to my profession?"

She stroked his face lovingly. "As long as you can satisfy me, you've got my vote."

In one swift move, she tore a strip from her ripped dress,

yanked his arms up over his head and tied them to the finial at the center of the bed's headboard, then mounted him. Just feeling her tighten around him sent shivers up his spine, made him rock hard and thick with desire—

Until he couldn't hold it back anymore, and exploded again.

"—*Mmmmm*...yeah," she whispered, "Like *that*..."

Ben didn't wake up until noon.

The first thing he remembered was that he was now officially running Mansfield's campaign. The second was that his new boss had told him that they'd all be taking off for New Year's Day.

Which led Ben to his third thought: how he could now spend that day off making love.

But first he'd have to find Red Velvet.

She wasn't in his bed. And a quick search of his townhouse proved that she wasn't in the shower, or kitchen or anywhere else within reach either.

However, he did find her note. In it, she apologized for having taken one of his tee shirts and a pair of sweat pants, along with a belt so they'd stay up around her.

It was signed *Maddy*.

No last name. No telephone number. Nothing that could allow him to find her.

So he forced himself to focus on creating a list of all that would have to be done quickly to build momentum for Mansfield, such as meeting and reviewing the current staffers the senator already had in place, calling in his own team of pollsters, webmasters, publicists and the likes, and of course vetting his candidate for any red flags—

But then his mind's eye envisioned Red Velvet Maddy dressed

in his gym clothes and tottering home on those ruby stilettos, and he got rock hard again.

CHAPTER 8

"Here's a first: Turns out your dude, Mansfield, is as clean as a whistle." Kenny Lafferty juggled his Subway sandwich, a family-sized bag of Doritos, and a 32-ounce bottle of Jolt into one hand as he tossed Ben a computer memory stick with the other. By his grimace, it was obvious that Kenny was disappointed. The private investigator prided himself on digging up filth, no matter how microscopic. Kenny's skullduggery allowed Ben to strategize how to handle whatever politicides needed to be spun—or buried even deeper. This time, though, he'd made a promise to himself: to walk away if in fact Mansfield proved too dirty.

"Bullshit. No way." Ben jammed the stick into one of his computer's USB ports and opened the first of what looked like hundreds of PDF files containing every public document, military record, media profile, press interview, job review and senatorial action made by, for and about one Andrew Jackson Mansfield. "Jesus, you even found his high school yearbook! What the hell did you do, Kenny, steal it out of his attic?"

Kenny almost choked on a Dorito. "You know I don't do B&E. Besides, I didn't have to—he donated it to his alma mater. All I had to do was pay the janitor to leave the trophy case open so we could 'borrow' it overnight, to scan."

"Unbelievable." Not Kenny's tactic, but Andy's high school history: Captain of the football team, not to mention Most Likely to Succeed; JROTC; and Valedictorian.

Ah, and the track team, too, just like me, thought Ben.

He stared down at Andy's senior picture. The face was thinner and unlined, but there was the same fierce determination in Andy's eyes.

"Yeah, and get a load of this," Kenny muttered. "Every single cheerleader—*on both squads*—wrote in his yearbook! 'Best kisser ever!' 'I LUV U 4-EVER!' 'I'll never forget you, Dandy Andy! XXX'. Damn. I couldn't even get a cheerleader to spit on me—"

"Any way to follow up on this stuff? I don't need another lothario on my hands." Five times burned, finally shy, was Ben's new mantra.

"I'm already on it, boss. Little Miss I LUV U, 4-EVER here"— he pointed to a photograph of one of the cheerleaders—a comely redhead doing a split for the camera—"grew up to become the school's principal. Unfortunately she's now also as broad as a barn door, and a real chatterbox, especially about her high school glory days. She says the senator kept his teammates in line, never picked on the nerds, and was always teacher's pet. As for his bedside manner, she swears that he was Mr. True Blue with his steadies. For sure he knew how to round the bases, if you catch my drift; but for the most part, he kept his dick in check. Or at least, in a raincoat. Ain't no li'l Dandy Andys gonna be poppin' up out of the North Carolina backwoods."

Ben frowned. It was all too good to be true. "Keep going."

As Kenny chugged his Jolt he opened another file with the computer's mouse, and clicked through its pages. "I'm telling you, the guy's a veritable saint. No stupid investments, no gambling debts, no secret college initiations, no sex addictions. Pays his taxes. Contributes to charity. And no My Lai Massacre from his Marine days. Mansfield's flyboy buddies sing tales of his derring-do. Hell, I was so hyped I almost enlisted myself. Then I remembered I'm afraid of heights."

With another click, the two-page spread from a fifteen-year-old *Washington Post* article on the Vandergalen-Mansfield wedding extravaganza appeared on the computer monitor. "After the Marines, Mansfield did his undergrad at UNC. Pre-Law, full scholarship; then law school at Yale, which is where he roomed with Paul Twist. Through Twist, he met his future wife, Abigail Jane Vandergalen. The rest is history."

The photo shoot had taken place in an elegant garden. Ben recognized it as Hillwood, the estate once owned by the wealthy Washington socialite, Marjorie Merriweather Post. Just off center in the spread was the loving couple. Abby, dressed in a frothy white wedding dress, faced the camera without her glasses. There was no joy in her blank stare. Was that the result of her myopia, or her shyness? From what he'd seen of her, Ben guessed the latter.

The wedding party—ten groomsmen, in white tie and tails posed with ten bridesmaids, all pretty, in pale pink¬—was arranged casually on and around the white wrought iron benches that were scattered about the lawn, while the ring bearer looked up the dresses of the two tiny flower girls.

Immediately Ben recognized the best man—Paul, although he was thinner, and sported a full head of hair. Ben scanned the faces of the others. One he recognized was now a judge in the Third Circuit of the U.S. Court of Appeals. Another headed a major investment firm. A third had cashed out from a Silicon Valley startup, and now ran a VC firm. Unlike Andy, all these men had come from money. Two other men were in Marine dress whites. The larger of the two, his flaming red hair cropped close to his scalp, was scowling.

I guess he didn't approve of his buddy's choice, Ben thought, as his eyes roamed to the woman next to the Marine—a brunette, who leaned into him suggestively while standing on her tiptoes in order to whisper in his ear. Certainly having a stunner like her on his arm should have eased his pain—

Damn she looks familiar...

Then Ben saw the beauty mark beside her mouth.

Maddy.

Granted, she was younger, sans bangs, and with longer hair that tumbled in loose coils below her slim shoulders. But yes, hell yes, he'd know her anywhere.

"—And best of all, no bimbo eruptions. If he's not on the senate floor, he's home with the wifey. Takes her to church on Sundays. Every Sunday, without fail. Go figure."

"Yeah yeah, great. Do we have IDs on everyone in this picture?"

"Yep. They're named there, in the photo credit. Except for the flyboys, they're all society types for the most part."

Ben scanned the copy, but it was too small, or his eyes were too bloodshot. And he was too impatient, anyway. "What about this one? Who's she?" Ben jabbed a finger at Maddy. "Zoom in so we can read it—"

"No need. I already know who she is. Madeline Elaine Vandergalen."

A Vandergalen? Oh...shit.

Ben took a deep breath. "She's—what, Abby's cousin or something?"

Kenny spewed his Jolt, he was laughing so hard. "Try sister."

"You have got to be kidding me." Ben wrenched the mouse from Kenny's hand and zoomed in on her face. Definitely there was a resemblance...

No, more than that. His eyes roamed back and forth between the two women, scrutinizing their chins, their noses, the slant of their cheekbones, those sad fathomless eyes.

Kenny's voice sounded a million miles away. "Seriously no joke. In fact, they're—"

"Twins." Ben could see it now, so easily. He closed his eyes, disgusted. At himself, at his luck. Or lack of it.

"Yeah. Hard to believe, eh? Though you wouldn't know it by looking at them now." Kenny clicked to another page, which showed a casual shot of the two, obviously taken last night, before Ben had arrived. They were seated at a table in the ballroom with Andy, Preston, some well-padded dowager whom Ben recognized as a renowned Republican donor, Paul, and a woman who must have been Paul's wife because he had his hand on her arm.

Abby smiled dutifully for the camera. But Maddy, unaware that her picture was being taken, looked forlorn. The chair beside Maddy was empty.

Maybe there really is an Invisible Man.

CHAPTER 9

As soon as Ben could, he shooed Kenny out the door. After realizing who Maddy was, he had stopped listening to him, anyway.

All he could think about was the fact that he'd fucked his candidate's sister-in-law.

And after being on the job, like, what—*an hour?*

Granted, that wasn't as bad as screwing a candidate's wife.

Yeah, just keep telling yourself that...

There was a separate background file on Abby, just as thick as Andy's. She and Maddy had been born into one of America's wealthiest aristocratic families, which meant that every offshoot of the Vandergalen family tree had been documented in society columns from Newport Beach to Palm Beach, not to mention the numerous profiles in *Fortune* and *Town & Country*.

Ben closed out the other files, and clicked through it page by page. The birth of the twins, to F. Bradford Vandergalen IV and his stately blond wife, the former Margaret "Missy" Alcott— Preston's only niece—was heralded in a *Washingtonian* article. An accompanying photo showed a strapping pretty boy. Platinum buzz cut. Steel hinge jaw. A tow-headed baby cradled on each strapping bicep. Except for the beehive, his wife was the spitting image of Abby. She sat at his loafered feet and looked up adoringly at her bronzed Adonis. Doing the math, Ben figured out that they'd been married exactly nine months to the day prior to the blessed births and rolled his eyes at that coincidence.

Another photo, taken at a charity Easter egg hunt, showed the golden-haired twins, now six, dressed in identical lace pinafores and white patent leather Mary Janes. Their arms were entwined and their smiles showed that each was missing two front teeth. The only telltale difference between them was the tiny dot to the left of Maddy's lip.

In a picture taken when they were eleven, the girls were thin, gawky, and wearing glasses. Still identically attired—albeit in the uniforms from the all-girl prep school, Ashcroft Academy—they wore their hair in similar chin-length pageboys. Clowning around, one leapfrogged over the other. Which was Maddy? He couldn't tell.

In the next picture they were fifteen. It was at the joint funeral of their parents, after a fatal automobile accident. The twins were mirror images: black reefers and wide-brimmed hats, their shoulders weighted under a mantle of grief. Apparently the photographer couldn't tell them apart either because the caption labeled them "the Vandergalen twins." A much younger Preston, with dark hair that had grayed only slightly at the temples, stood on their right, his face set in a stoic grimace. Beside him was a woman—younger, and with the same aquiline features. Ben presumed she was his sister. The accompanying article confirmed this: "The girls now reside with their great aunt, Phoebe Lavinia Alcott, at Asquith Hall, the Alcott ancestral estate, in rural Virginia."

By the time their high school graduation pictures were taken, the girls looked radically different from each other: The doe-eyed Abby had held onto her glasses and her gawkiness, but now it was coupled with a grim sadness. The caption beneath the photo said: "Next stop: Sarah Lawrence, as an art history major."

Whereas she'd stayed at Ashcroft, Maddy, now kohl-eyed,

raven-haired, and sporting rings in her brow and nose, had somehow ended up at Occoquan's local public high school. A tight, white t-shirt, sheer enough to expose a black low-cut push-up bra, had replaced the staid school uniform. Her eyes, no longer shielded by glasses, pierced the camera with blatant defiance.

And they were the same startling blue hue as Abby's.

She wears contacts now, thought Ben. It makes the transition complete. For whatever reason, she doesn't want to be a twin. Or at least, she doesn't want to be Abby's twin.

He could imagine why. Abby would always be the good girl.

CHAPTER 10

At first he tried to convince himself that he had nothing to worry about. It had been a one-night stand, nothing more. Otherwise she would have left him some way to get in touch with her. And so what if, somewhere down the line, they ran into each other. Hell, she probably wouldn't even remember him...

Fat chance. Even if the twins weren't as close as they once were, one thing was sure: Maddy was still close enough to Abby to attend a big fundraiser in her brother-in-law's honor. And if that were the case, then odds were she'd already boasted to Abby about her latest conquest: Andy's new political consultant.

And considering Andy's true blue nature, Ben would be back out on the street.

That thought made his skin crawl.

You're being paranoid. Of course she'll keep her mouth shut. And if not, cross that bridge when you come to it.

He worked until midnight, then flopped into bed, exhausted. He tried not to think about it, but Maddy filled his dreams.

The vision seemed real enough, caught there in the moonlight streaming through his bedroom window. The sight of her took his breath away. Not because she was naked, but because she was so beautiful, even more than he remembered.

Only when she grazed his lips with hers did he truly believe she was there with him.

"How did you get in?" He should have been cross. Certainly not aroused and aching.

She laughed that husky, honeyed chuckle that made his groin ache in anticipation every time he heard it. "Silly Ben! Everyone leaves a key under the mat. Or, like you, above the door sill." She dangled his key playfully then tossed it to him before sliding under the sheet next to him, cuddling up to his chest.

Angrily, he sat up. With all he wanted to say to her, all he could manage to stammer out was: "So...you're *her* twin? Why didn't you tell me?"

That had her laughing. "I was wondering when you'd find out." The sheet drifted off her breast as she propped herself up on one elbow. "I guess because it doesn't mean anything."

"Just what do you mean by that? For Christ sakes, you're Andy's sister-in-law, and I'm running his campaign! Look, Maddy, if I had known—"

"What? What would you have done? Would you have quit fucking me, Ben?"

My candidate's sister-in-law? Yeah, I would have quit—

Hell no. Who am I kidding?

Not Maddy. The look on her face told him so. God, he wanted her even now.

As if reading his mind she reached down and put her hand on his crotch.

He almost exploded.

She smiled triumphantly.

As badly as he wanted to take her right then and there, he grabbed her wrist and yanked it away. "What, are you crazy? Let's not forget that I can lose my job over this little incident of mistaken identity! What if Preston, or Paul—or God forbid, *your sister*—had seen us making out in the lobby—"

"What if they had seen you, practically raping me in the

elevator?" She pressed a long tapered finger to her lips in mock shock. "Frankly, I think they would have been jealous."

"This is no laughing matter, Maddy." He closed his eyes to clear his mind of the image that had popped into it: his hand, tearing at the seam of Maddy's red velvet gown as it made its way to the warm thigh beneath it. "I guess what I'm trying to say is that—well, this isn't going to work out." *And no one is sadder about that than me.*

"You're wrong. It works perfectly, because neither of us wants this relationship to go public. And it shouldn't. Ben, seriously, it has nothing to do with anyone but us. That is, if we want to stay fuck buddies."

Fuck buddies. Ben couldn't believe his ears. Keeping it on the lowdown, with no obligations, no drama? Tantalizing...

"Interesting proposition. Not to look a gift horse in the mouth or anything, but do you mind me telling why you don't want anyone to know about us?"

"Because it's no one else's business. Ben, you have no idea what it's like to be a Vandergalen. The one thing I want more than anything—anonymity—I can't have, because of my name. Frankly, that's why you and I are perfect for each other. And not just in the obvious way." She cast her eyes lovingly at his cock. "Besides, Andy needs you on his team. Don't you think I know that? Don't you think I want that for him—and for Abby? If he wins, we all do. So let's just keep things spontaneous. You know, friends with benefits. It's more fun that way, isn't it?"

"But don't you think it'll be somewhat awkward when we run into each other at his political events? I know it will be for me."

"You know better than anyone what Andy's schedule will be like, from now until the end of primaries. Look, I'll make it easy for you. I just won't go to any." Her face hardened. "Abby won't expect me there, anyway. We aren't that close. We lead very different lives."

The pictures in Kenny's file were proof of that.

Ben sighed. Seriously, if they both kept their mouths shut, what was the downside? In hindsight, it was flattering to think that she was the one trying to keep their relationship under wraps so that his job wouldn't be jeopardized—

But he knew better than that. Whatever her reasons were, he couldn't fathom them now, not with her hands roaming between his thighs, cupping his balls...

By the time she knelt down and took him in her mouth, he could care less about her reason for secrecy. He had already forgiven her.

CHAPTER 11

"I just *looooove* that man," cooed the legs-up-to-there single-mommy Bally's showgirl to her much shorter gal pal, the croupier from the MGM Grand. "Deep down in my heart, I truly believe that we'll finally get universal healthcare if he's elected."

Her friend shushed her loudly. But Ben, who was standing just behind the women, gave a silent prayer of thanks. And they weren't the only ones enthralled with what they were hearing from Senator Andrew Jackson Mansfield at the candidate's town hall meeting there in the Clark County Library's large theater. Ben flipped through the 399 reservation profile cards so that he could match names and occupations to those who sat in the seat numbers around the two women. The faces that went with the cards he chose—five self-employeds, three housewives, and a long distance trucker—were also nodding involuntarily as they leaned forward to catch each inspiring word.

Because Andy Mansfield was on fire.

Like a Baptist preacher at a revival meeting, Andy's voice, nuanced with compassion, filled the auditorium with the strength of his conviction. "In recent years, my friends, we have witnessed drastic changes—affecting our jobs, our environment, and our personal lives."

Without missing a beat, he took the cordless microphone with him as he strolled off the stage in order to pace up and down the broad aisle that divided the auditorium. "But while the world changes around us, our leaders have stood still. Answer this: Which leaders inspire our nation and lead us to the good deeds that need to be done? We have seen Washington grow small-minded and mean-spirited as our politics have devolved and our goals have dissolved. But of course it doesn't have to be this way."

He then paused in front of a young couple. Taking their hands in his own, he nudged them to rise so that they stood with him. "But real change comes from *people*. Citizens like you, and like me, who demand more of government, and who recognize that educating our children and securing the benefits of modern healthcare for rich and poor alike are of greater importance than the politics of greed and personal gain."

Victoriously, he raised their hands high. "With me as your president, you'll have the government you deserve." The whole room rose, clapping and hooting, and Ben along with it. The crowd's adoration was contagious.

Listen to them, Ben thought. If the primaries were held today, he'd win. No contest.

"You're some lucky dog, ain't you now? Your man there is pure gold." The good ol' boy growling into Ben's earpiece was Eddie Klein, the renowned ad man. The very first person recruited by Ben for Team Mansfield, Ed had come with a couple of cameramen to tape some man-of-the-people crowd shots. From them he would mold the senator's vision into simple market-specific soundbites, and see that the public was hit over the head with it every time they turned on their TV or logged onto their computers.

Ben looked up to the control booth above and behind the audience, and gave Eddie a thumbs-up. Hell yeah, Andy was golden. A god among men.

And he'd soon be the next President of the United States.

In a whirlwind six days—just in time for Ben and Andy's first eleven-city road trip together—Ben had hobbled together a fairly decent staff that included twenty-five paid professionals, plus another ten volunteers. Besides Eddie for advertising and Kenny for background and due diligence, there was Jilly O'Connor, a seasoned press secretary whose blunt honesty kept her on the good side of reporters and pundits.

And there was Spike Levine, the pollster who had revolutionized the industry when he took registration-based sampling one step further by marrying it to a software program that searched voters' credit card charges for items reflecting hot button issues such as healthcare, education, gun control, gasoline, and philanthropies, giving his polls an accuracy level of plus-or-minus one percent.

Ben had also wrangled retired Air Force Major General Carver Elson, and former Secretary of State John Parks, as Andy's foreign-policy advisers. Elson would rally other high profile experts into a fluid advisory team that would always be at the senator's fingertips. Parks joined Mansfield's road show. An A-Team of economic advisors was also set up, including economists, former CEOs of various financial institutions, even a former Secretary of the Treasury. They all had one thing in common: they abhorred Talbot's neocon-driven agenda. "His BS is dividing the party, and putting our soldiers in harm's way unnecessarily," growled Elson.

Of course Paul Twist was the campaign's finance chair. And he had already hired Terry Loehman to spearhead the big-ticket fundraisers in key markets. Terry was to be aided by his longtime partner Pat, a professional event planner. Both had Ben's admiration.

The biggest recruiting coup was convincing the renowned Mallory sisters, Bess and Tess, to run Mansfield's ground war: that is, organize and rally the senator's national volunteer corps by precincts, districts and states. But Ben could take no credit for that win. Democratic stalwarts through and through, initially they had declined his invitation to hop the fence. What it took was a one-on-one meeting with Andy. After hearing his heartfelt no-holds-barred pitch, they readily jumped onboard.

"Dreamy," was what Tess called him. Or was it Bess? Ben could never tell the roly-poly gray-haired sisters apart.

Like now, as one of them corralled some eager audience members for the Q&A lineup. Which twin was holding the mike? Not that it mattered. At that very moment, all that counted was the adoration for Andy in the participants' eyes.

The first one up, a bookstore employee named Cindy, was so awed and nervous that Ben winced as she wrangled with the squirming baby in her arms. "I work a full-time job, my husband works two. Still we can't make ends meet! And none of our jobs offer healthcare for 'part-time' employees. Not to mention that the cost of food and gas just keeps going up! When do we become the priority of our government?"

A chorus of "Ahhhh" echoed through the theater as Andy took the child from its mother and rocked it on his shoulder. "Even in Kitty Hawk, the small town where I grew up, we knew our neighbors, and as a community we recognized that we were only as strong as those who were most in need. Of course back then we had a middle class. Today we have the haves and the have-nots. And yet, we can't afford to ignore the needs of the many for the financial gains of the few. Cindy, that's not my North Carolina. And that's not my America. Nor is it yours."

Still cradling her child, Andy put an arm around Cindy. Through his earpiece, Ben heard Eddie shout "Fucking A! That's the money shot..." In his mind's eye, Ben could see the TV ad already. Andy's closing comments made it all that much better:

"Together we can change that, and restore the American dream—where every hardworking individual has the opportunity to achieve, to see their children's dreams succeed. So the short answer to your question as to when you become your government's priority: It's my first day in the Oval Office."

As one, the crowd jumped to its feet, but this time it stayed there, stomping and chanting "An-*dy*! An-*dy*! An-*dy*..."

Ben, too, chanted along with the crowd. Andy didn't just woo potential voters. He inspired them. And he never sidestepped a hot issue with a pat answer. Instead he gave them the unvarnished truth, backed up by statistics that flowed easily off the tip of his tongue.

Best yet, he did it standing side-by-side with them, looking them in the eye, letting them know that he was accessible. That he was one of them.

For the first time in over a decade, Ben actually *liked* one of his candidates.

CHAPTER 12

The feeling was mutual. Ben found that out when they landed back in Washington and Andy asked if he'd join him for a late night drink at his favorite dive bar, a pool hall called Bedrock Billiards, to meet the men he called "my brothers, the only guys I can trust."

The group was small but choice. Besides Paul Twist, who had already shed his very expensive Savile Row suit jacket and loosened his Armani tie, its only other member was a man Andy introduced as Fred Hanover.

"Fred and I served together in the Marine Corps," Andy explained. "We met during a six-month deployment to Iwakuni. I was his section leader. Now Fred is at Langley."

Bulky and slack-jawed, Fred could easily have passed as one of the dozen or so old school frat boys slouched over the pool hall's vintage bright cherry leather barstools, watching the Capitols getting out-skated by the Hurricanes. Except for one thing: his eyes scanned the pool hall constantly, roaming over faces, taking in every random move. No doubt he had watched Ben as he got his bearings in the crowded, darkly lit room and maneuvered over to them.

Ben immediately recognized Fred from the *Washingtonian* article on the Mansfields' wedding: he was the redheaded groomsman who had stood beside Maddy.

So now he's CIA, thought Ben.

After crunching Ben's hand in his massive fist, Fred busied himself with racking balls for a game of Eight-Ball. In the meantime Paul signaled the waitress for a round of beers.

She was adorable, a Kewpie doll with strawberry curls and a chest that filled out her tight black tee-shirt to the stretching point. By the way she batted her thick lashes at Andy, it was obvious that she recognized him. But other than a formal nod when she placed a Flying Dog on his coaster, he didn't give her a second glance.

As she walked off, Fred elbowed Paul, who sighed, pulled out his wallet and handed over a dollar bill.

Ben raised an eyebrow. "What was that for?"

Fred chuckled. "No big deal. Just a little bet we have going. Andy attracts girls like a flower attracts bees. But I've yet to see him even look twice at another woman. Years ago Paul here was stupid enough to call my bluff. I'd say that, by the end of this election, I'll have enough money to retire from my day job."

Andy pretended to concentrate on his shot, but he smiled just the same. When the cue ball smacked into two striped balls, they hurdled off into separate corner pockets.

That a boy. Keep your eyes on the prize.

Ben knew too many politicians whose tastes for bedfellows were both strange and insatiable. What was Abby's hold over her husband, her bankability or her bedside manner?

For whatever reason, she hadn't been able to make the Las Vegas trip with them, so he hadn't had an opportunity to observe her himself, let alone thank her for suggesting him for the job.

Feeling Ben's eyes on him, Andy laughed. "You seem positively relieved, Brinker. Hey, I don't blame you, after what you've been through." He tossed Ben the cue stick. "What can I say? Abby is one in a million. I don't know what I ever did to deserve her. I mean, look at all she's doing so that I get elected. With all I know about this rotten world, I guess I'm a fool to run." He looked Ben straight in the eye. "But Abby believes—and I do, too—that we can save this planet before we push it to the point of no return. It's why we have to win."

Ben shrugged. "Global warming, the environment—they're all great campaign issues—"

"No. You don't get it. This is more than that…" He stopped, at a loss for words. "Look, Ben, do you fly?"

Ben laughed. "Sure, back in tourist. It's the quickest way to get from point A to point B."

"Agreed. I guess that's the goal in everything we do in life, right?" Andy stared out into the pool hall, his eyes sweeping over the crowd that was cheering a last minute save by the Capitols' goalie. "As for me—well, I fly because I love it. In the cockpit, surrounded by a sound set of wings, a competent pilot is truly in command of his own destiny. Any journey is what you make of it. And, if you follow the waypoints, you'll never lose your way."

"Waypoints? What are those?"

"Landmarks you've identified beforehand, that will guide you to your destination. As long as you keep them in your sights, you'll stay on the right path." He paused. "All the paths we aim for in life have very clear markers. But sometimes, when we think we know it all, we ignore them. We look for shortcuts. That's when we run off-course. And into trouble. If it weren't for Abby, I'd be so far off track! She keeps me on the straight and narrow. She is my angel."

Andy's angel.

Long ago Ben had noted that a politician's wife fell into one of two categories: either she had an opinion on everything and made a nuisance of herself, or you had to drag her along for the ride, kicking and screaming.

Abby's innate shyness put her in the latter category.

Rarely did a politician's wife realize that the best place for her in the vast scheme of things was at her husband's side, smiling demurely—but only for the photo op. Afterward, between elections, she was free to slip offstage, where she could enjoy her reward for playing the game so well—the perks that came with his power.

Whether she used the perks for her own personal pleasure or for some worthy cause was between her and her conscience—that is, as long as any press she garnered was good for her husband.

Better yet, she should avoid the press altogether. Except during election season, obviously.

Thank God the campaign was just now gearing up. But the way Andy was already breathing down Talbot's neck, Abby's absence from the campaign trail would become an issue sooner than later.

Ben couldn't help but think about Maddy. Was she truly a part of his future, perhaps his angel?

I guess it's too early to tell.

"Seems that we're already rattling a few important cages. We just got a big donation from Tully Broadbent, the high-tech entrepreneur. He's never veered from the party favorite. That's causing the old boys a shit fit." Paul's breaking shot slammed the balls into every corner of the pool table. The nine ball fell into a pocket, as did the thirteen. He pumped his fist then took a swig of his Guinness.

"I guess it helps that good ol' Tully and I were both Leathernecks." Andy grinned slyly. "I'm sure if Talbot could do it over again, he would have signed up during Vietnam, instead of begging for a deferment."

It was Ben's turn to shrug. "I'm not so sure about that, Senator. If the past has taught us anything, it's not what you did, but how you spin it."

"We're among friends, here, Ben. Please, call me Andy."

"I'd be honored." He tipped his glass toward the senator.

Paul's next shot was a miss. It was Fred's turn up to shoot. "I'm guessing their grumbling has more to do with your very vocal stance against the president's Venezuelan policy."

What looked like an easy shot ricocheted off another ball, missing the pocket by mere millimeters. Maybe that had something to do with the fact that Fred had been watching the door out of the corner of his eye.

Either this guy never turns it off, or this place isn't as secure as Andy thinks.

"The way things are going, his call to arms—or maybe I should say his boondoggle—will cost a lot of soldiers their lives. I can't let that happen." Andy's drawl was nonchalant, but Ben knew better. "It's going to cost him votes, too. In any regard, I'm through kowtowing to those dinosaurs." He tapped Ben's shoulder with his stick then set up his shot. "And with Ben at the helm, I'll have the one thing I need to win: the support of the voters." Andy popped the five ball into a corner pocket, and followed it up by sinking the three ball on a bank shot into the side.

Ben was flattered at the compliment. Still, Paul's involuntary frown indicated that as far as he was concerned, the jury was still out on Ben.

Jeez, and I thought this numbnuts was going to cut me some slack.

Paul didn't seem too friendly with Fred either. The feeling must have been mutual since neither had exchanged more than a word or two throughout the whole game. Both were close to Andy, but obviously they didn't think much of each other.

The game ended about the same time their pizza arrived. Fred waited until they were seated to divulge some important information: there had been an upsurge in terrorist chatter.

"But the sources seem suspicious. Not the usual channels. In fact, I suspect it's the work of Talbot's Ghost Squad. The timing is just too perfect." He gulped down one piece, then grabbed another.

Mansfield pushed away his plate. "I wouldn't doubt that in the least."

"What do you mean by his 'Ghost Squad'?" asked Ben.

Paul laughed uneasily. "It's part of Fred's interdepartmental paranoia. He thinks Talbot has inside guys at the defense agencies—Homeland Security, CIA, FBI, ATF—spying within their own organizations and reporting back to him." He grabbed a second slice of pizza. "Trust me, Fred, the man spends too much time on the golf course to play *I Spy* in his spare time."

Fred took a swig of his beer. "He came out of Langley, remember? Once a spook, always a spook. No matter what he does now, he learned enough there to make it work for him when the time came—like now that he's running for the presidency. And I can't be the only one who finds it a little suspicious that the press has picked up his mantra about 'liberating the Venezuelan people from that authoritarian madman, Padilla' just a ¬few weeks after Padilla kicked Talbot's Petrochem buddies out of the country, then pulled a Chavez and nationalized all the oil fields. For that reason alone they need Talbot to win this election."

"Morals and freedom aside, Venezuela sells sixty percent of its oil to us. That translates into a million and a half barrels a day. When Padilla was playing nice, it was easy—and cheap¬—to get it," explained Andy. Then he laughed. "I'm sure Talbot's asshole puckered up when he heard about Padilla's meeting with the Chinese, to sign an even bigger oil accord than last year's." He looked over at Fred. "Hey, do me a favor and keep an eye on that chatter. If it's what you suspect, I'll need proof, at all costs."

Andy sat on the Armed Services Committee, the Senate Committee on Homeland Security and Government Affairs, and the Select Committee on Intelligence. More than that, he made it a point to track down discrepancies in what these committees were told in white papers, and to talk to the people in the field firsthand.

In other words, if Andy smells a rat, there is one to be found, thought Ben.

Fred grimaced, the first sign of emotion Ben had seen on his face. "Dude, between your senate hearings and your campaigning, you're not exactly easy to track down."

"That's life. Hey, if you can't find me, then find my boy here." Andy pointed to Ben.

Fred didn't even respond to that. Obviously he wasn't any more convinced than Paul that Ben deserved their trust.

CHAPTER 13

Then again, maybe I don't deserve their trust.

That realization came to Ben later that very night, as he held Maddy in his arms.

As hot as the sex was with Maddy, the fact that their post-coital conversations were inevitably about the campaign was also a turn-on to him. Sex and politics were his two favorite pastimes. Either she was she his fantasy fuck, or she was too good to be true.

His dick voted for the former.

In fact, he was about to tell her some of the ideas that Eddie Klein's creative team had already come up with for Andy's video web ads. But then he remembered the suspicious look Fred had given him and stopped talking in mid-sentence.

Unfortunately for him, Maddy paused too—she'd been circling his nipple with her tongue—and looked up at him. "What's wrong?"

"Nothing, really. I—I'm just tired." With both hands, he gently lifted her onto his chest so that he could look her in the eye. "No, that's not true. I guess what I'm trying to say is that we always seem to talk about me. Or at least, my job."

She smirked. "You're not boring me, trust me. In fact, I find what you do fascinating."

"Yeah? And why is that?" He tried to keep the suspicion out of his voice.

"Because Andy—and you—are out there, making a difference."

"You're an artist. You make a difference, too."

She rolled off of him and onto her side. Her ass was leaning against his thigh. They were both hot and sticky, and the sheet had fallen somewhere near the foot of the bed. Silhouetted in starlight, the dip between her shoulder and hip beckoned him to cradle her, but he held back, although he could feel his cock rising to the occasion yet again.

"Sure, I create things that make people stop and think. At least I hope they do. But it's not the same," she murmured. "You— he—take people one step further. They're inspired to *act*."

How about you? He wanted to ask her, *Are you acting now?*

But he didn't. Instead he asked: "What were you doing there, the night we met?"

"Where...at the Fairmont?"

"Yes. Why were you there?" He knew he should have sat up, but with his hard-on leading him to her, he'd forget all he wanted to ask—all he *should* have asked—weeks ago.

"I was invited. Remember?" Maddy sounded annoyed. She flipped over onto her stomach and turned her head so that it faced away from him and toward the wall. Because she was slightly spread-eagled, a dainty lacquered toe gently grazed his ankle.

He nearly came right then and there.

When he came to his senses, he croaked out: "Had you arrived with someone?"

"No." Her voice was muffled, a million miles away.

She's lying.

"Who is—the Invisible Man?"

Dead silence.

"Was he there that night?"

Instead of answering him, she got up out of bed, collected the clothes she'd strewn around the room and headed to the bathroom. He groaned at the thought of losing her—both in his bed that very minute, and out of it for the rest of his life.

Jesus, why am I being so paranoid? Because of Spooky Fred? Well, fuck that shit...

Ben could hear the shower running. He forced himself to get up. When he knocked, there was no answer, but she hadn't locked the door so he opened it and peeked inside.

The steam had already enveloped the room, and he could make her out through the beveled shower door.

She was sobbing.

He wrapped himself around her and held her like that for what seemed an eternity. Or at least long enough for the water to go from scalding hot, like she had it, to tepidly cool. It made them both shiver, which made her laugh finally, which made him want to kiss her—

But she kissed him first.

By the time they came up for air, the water was ice cold. But instead of leaving the shower, he got behind her, tilting her forward just enough so that she had to hold onto the tile and stand tall on those beautiful toes he loved so dearly while he thrust deep inside of her, cupping her breasts and her taut nipples with his wrinkled fingertips.

Afterward they fell into his bed, still wet.

He was shaving in the bathroom and she was getting dressed in the bedroom when her cell phone chirped. He pretended to be looking in the mirror at a sideburn, but in truth he was watching her when, instead of picking up, she noted the Caller ID, then muted the ringer.

"Why didn't you answer it?"

She looked up startled, then smiled coyly. "Because it's my sugar daddy."

But Ben wasn't laughing. "Maddy, I tell you everything. But I know virtually nothing about you. What, is it Mr. Invisible?"

"Jesus, Ben! Get real."

"I am being real."

"Then, *for real*, it's none of your business."

"I want to make it my business." He laid down his razor and wiped off the last few wisps of shaving cream with the back of his hand. "Maddy, sweetheart, I want you all to myself."

"Forget it, Ben. I like things just the way they are."

"You mean that you want to stay fuck buddies?"

"Sure. Why not?" Maddy picked up her bra then turned her back on him as she hooked it. Her way of saying END OF STORY.

"I don't get it. Why can't we take this—this *whatever* it is—to the next step?"

She quit buttoning her blouse and sighed. "Ben, it's not happening, ever. And if you push it, you'll lose me. For good."

She went into the bathroom and slammed the door.

He waited until she turned on the blow dryer before pulling her cell phone from her purse and reading the Caller ID: *Anonymous.*

Of course, he could just hit redial and see who picked up...

But he didn't. Because she was right.

There was no way in hell he'd risk losing her.

CHAPTER 14

Manolo Padilla's personal physician, Jorge Leon, was considered the rising star of Venezuela's medical community. He was young and handsome. He had graduated at the top of his class at St. George's, University of London. And most importantly, he was devoted to Padilla's policies, without question.

That might have had something to do with the fact that he was married to Padilla's niece, Lina.

It was because Lina was pregnant that Jorge was an easy mark. Two heartbeats in the womb meant twins—as it turns out, a boy and a girl. Lina's difficulty in getting pregnant meant lots of bed rest, and little activity outside their gated Caracas estate. And her bodyguard's boredom with a job that required nothing more of him than to drive Señora Leon to her doctor's office once a week allowed for easy entry.

All Smith's men had to do was take over the delivery truck from Bongo International on the day that the babies' cribs were to be delivered. (Since they had been ordered from that capitalist retail behemoth, Pottery Barn Kids, Smith felt this was apropos.)

The bodyguard was taken out with one shot to the forehead. Lina whimpered, but she did not struggle while Smith's men tied her up and hustled her into the back of the truck.

Then a call was made to Dr. Leon, at his office. The message, delivered by Smith, was simple: No phone calls to Padilla's security people. Smith would know if he did, because Jorge was already being tailed, and his office and home were bugged. The next morning the good doctor was to take the first *telefericos*—one of the colorful cable cars that transported tourists up to the peak of *Cerro el Avila.*

All Jorge needed to hear was Lina sobbing incoherently into the phone to know that Smith meant business.

Smith had arranged for them to be alone as the cable car dangled high above bustling Caracas on that warm cloudless morning. The view—from the translucent sea and khaki beaches to the bustling city below and the verdant jungle beyond—was truly awe-inspiring. But Jorge's sad dark eyes never left Smith's face, except when he was handed the small black box that enclosed a syringe. Jorge was not told what the syringe contained, only that he should tell Padilla that there was an irregularity in his heartbeat, and that some tests had to be run to determine how serious it was. An MRI would be scheduled. Then right before the MRI, Jorge would inject the drug in Padilla, along with the usual contrast agents. A heart attack would be induced once the syringe's contents mixed with the other drugs.

By the time the autopsy was done, all traces of the killing agent will have disappeared.

When the official announcement of Padilla's death was heralded, Lina would be released, right then and there.

Jorge nodded to demonstrate his understanding of what was to be done.

Even before the cable car crested the summit, Jorge had weighed all his options and concluded the following:

He could tell Padilla of the gringo's plan, but then Lina would die before they found her captors.

Worse yet, Padilla would blame Jorge for Lina's abduction, and rail at him for meeting with Smith without the dictator's knowledge. Then to make an example of him and avenge his niece and her unborn babies, Padilla would order him shot for his ill-fated decisions.

Or he could follow through on Smith's perfect plan, customized specifically for Padilla's trusted doctor and nephew-in-law.

But Jorge had looked in the gringo devil's eyes, and what he saw there told him that Smith would never release his Lina. That Jorge would never hold her in his arms again.

That his children would never be born.

And so, as the cable car hung in mid air, he wrenched open the door and jumped to his death.

With God's forgiveness, he would be waiting for his family in heaven.

The doctor's choice did not surprise Smith. After all, the man was smart. So yes, all of his deductions had been right on the mark.

No problem. Now Talbot would be forced to see the merit of Plan B.

By the time they had identified the suicidal jumper as the esteemed Doctor Leon, Lina's body had already been found in her bathtub, her wrists slit.

CHAPTER 15

Maddy's way of punishing Ben's impudence was to appear at will, and only when he least expected it. But he'd learned his lesson and never again questioned her comings and goings.

Instead, he tried hard not to think about her, not to wonder if she was going to be waiting for him when he got home from work. Needless to say he was glad when the Mansfield campaign hit the road again. He welcomed the chance to get out of town, to focus on something other than the fact that he was so obviously pussywhipped.

Andy's speech in Iowa, encouraging farmers to unite in their efforts to make biofuels, wave and wind resources the primary fuel source for the country, was a big hit. *Newsweek* showed up to cover it, calling his white paper on the issue "both user friendly and business friendly. Senator Mansfield will have the other candidates going green, too—with envy..."

Two days later, the latest NBC/*Wall Street Journal* poll came out, showing the senator within spitting distance of Talbot.

Ben and Andy got the news from Sukie while they were flying back from a stopover in Chicago, where three back-to-back fundraisers there were projected to net the campaign a tidy two million dollars. Abby was to rendezvous with them at the Four Seasons.

They watched Brian Williams' newscast about the poll from

the satellite broadcast feed on the campaign's private jet. Afterward, the anchorman segued into a biographical piece on Andy: the fact that Mansfield was the son of an itinerate farmer and a housewife; that he was orphaned at sixteen and raised himself, then enlisted as a Marine flight jock after high school; that as a pilot he had performed numerous acts of heroism; how, after leaving the Marines, Andy had gone onto law school and become a public defender; how he'd even won a case before the Supreme Court; a laundry list accounting of his accomplishments as a U.S. senator; and finally, his storybook marriage to a Vandergalen heiress.

It was a veritable love letter. "Some are already saying that this kind of enthusiasm for a candidate has not been seen since Barack Obama's first term," intoned Williams. "Early polls are showing that the senator is one of those rare candidates who attracts voters from across party lines."

The staffers on the plane with Andy and Ben—Tess, Bess, and Jilly among them—showed their approval with hoots and high-fives. The handful of reporters who'd hitched a ride on the plane in order to cover the senator while he was on the campaign trail nodded and grinned as they scribbled copious notes.

That piece was followed by a pundit analysis of Mansfield's campaign. Williams' guests for the segment were the new Republican National Committee chairman James Orkin, and the conservative *New York Times* columnist, David Brooks. Williams asked Orkin point blank if the GOP's leaders considered Mansfield's surge in the polls "something that the party could get behind."

"Brian, we stand behind all our candidates," Orkin chuckled. "But at this time, I think you'd agree with me that your question may be somewhat premature. Remember, there's another twelve months to go before the first primary. No doubt about it, Andy's a good man—but at this stage of his career, he lacks the gravitas of the frontrunner, Vice President Talbot."

Andy snorted loudly at that.

Brooks chimed in, "You know, in past presidential races, others have had impressive early leads. Remember Howard Dean in '04? And Mike Huckabee in '08? What's going to matter now is whether or not Senator Mansfield can keep up the momentum. It will help him immensely if he has a good team around him. Unfortunately, I question whether that's the case. Hiring campaign strategist Ben Brinker, if you ask me, was a somewhat questionable move."

Williams raised an eyebrow. "Why is that, David?"

Brooks shrugged. "Brinker's past experience has been exclusively with Democratic candidates. That's not to say that consultants can't play both sides of the fence, but it does say something about Mansfield's inability to attract a campaign adviser who knows the policies, platforms, and players within his own party."

"Not to mention that Brinker's last three candidates have been embroiled in some pretty serious scandals," Orkin chimed in.

Williams nodded sagely. "Most recently, the Congressman Calder love child incident."

"Exactly." Orkin shook his head sadly. "So you have to ask yourself why Mansfield would even dare associate himself with that kind of—oh, I don't know, I guess you'd call it 'bad campaign karma.' He can't afford to do anything that reflects poorly on his ability to make the right choices, particularly during this very important 'exploratory' time period."

The other two men nodded in agreement.

"That said, I can't help but think that the two of them, Talbot and Mansfield, would make a dream ticket for the party—"

Andy clicked the remote so that the screen went black. "Me, on the ticket with Talbot? Hell, I wouldn't run a three-legged race with that bastard."

"What Orkin just said proves that they're running scared," Ben said.

"They should be," Andy added. "Because I'm pulling this off. We're pulling this off." As he said that, he looked each member of his staff in the eye. When he got to Ben, he gave him a knowing grin and a thumbs-up. Ben appreciated it. He had flinched when Orkin all but called him an albatross around the senator's neck.

They're circling the wagons, he thought. It's time to pull out some heavier ammo. Like Abigail.

Even a timid wife at Andy's side was better than none.

CHAPTER 16

The front desk confirmed that yes, Mrs. Mansfield was already checked into the Senator's suite. But before Andy could join her, a *Sun-Times* political reporter buttonholed him.

"Hey, Ben, go upstairs and tell Abby I'll be up as soon as I can, will you? While you're at it, you can fill her in on Iowa."

Ben double-checked the senator's room number with the reservation desk. The reservationist explained that she'd put the Mansfields in the presidential suite. The senator had insisted that Ben have a suite next to his.

"Fine with me," Ben murmured. Taking the electronic room key she handed him he grabbed his suitcase and headed for the elevator.

The suite opened into an elegant living room. It was much larger than he'd expected, and certainly much grander. The first door he opened was a galley kitchen. Sweet, but overkill. The next opened into a closet. Granted it was large enough to sleep in, but there was no bed, so he knew it wasn't the bedroom. Then he saw the hallway. He was halfway down it when he heard a murmur of voices.

Intrigued he glanced through the double entry door—

Apparently the desk clerk had coded his key with the wrong room number, because the woman speaking was Abby. She was standing beside the bed: her skirt unzipped and hugging her hips, her blouse opened and bra exposed to some man—tall, thin, regal looking¬–who had his hand on her arm. She was intent on what he was saying. So intent that neither of them realized that Ben was staring at them.

He slipped away before they saw him, backing down the hallway and out of the suite, gently closing the door behind him.

He waited until he got to the elevator before cursing.

At least he refrained from punching a hole in the wall.

CHAPTER 17

So Abby, *the perfect senator's wife*, was having an affair.

Ben Brinker, who was never off balance even when confronted by the Washington press corps, was suddenly numb, his mouth dry as wood, his hands damp and cold with perspiration. He contemplated the damage that could be done to the campaign, should anyone find out.

Andy would be made a laughing stock.

And Ben would be without a candidate, once again.

What was it Chris Matthews had called him? Oh yeah—a political cooler.

Well, this latest bit of bad luck proved it. Once again he'd chosen the wrong candidate.

The elevator announced its presence with muted chimes.

"Hold it, please."

Ben looked up to see the man—*Abby's lover*—trotting down the hall toward him, briefcase at his side. Too stunned to do anything but nod mutely, Ben stood beside the man as the elevator doors opened—

Inside was Andy with one of the Mallory twins, who was hazing the bellhop for dragging the senator's bags.

"Hey, have you seen her yet?" Andy fairly bounded out of the elevator. For some strange reason press interviews energized him. As he glanced from Ben to the other man, Ben froze in horror. Did he know the guy? And if so, did he know the man's role in Abby's life?

Apparently not. They barely exchanged glances as the man hurried into the elevator and disappeared as the door slid shut.

"The state chair is bringing Fleischer Daley with him. Should make a great photo op. Jilly is already on it. Which reminds me: you'd mentioned—" By the time Ben got his bearings, Andy was already halfway down the hall. Ben walked back through the suite's door just in time to see Andy take Abby's hand and kiss it ever so sweetly. But she avoided his eyes, choosing to look down at the floor instead.

Why, you two-faced bitch. I guess you and Maddy have more in common than people realize.

But at least Maddy's honest about wanting to play the field.

Suddenly there was a long silence and Ben realized they were staring at him, waiting for him to respond. He knew that he should say something, anything, but the words stuck in his throat. Instead he nodded. Finally he was able to stutter out some sort of acknowledgment, all the while inching back toward the door.

But then, hesitantly, Abby extended her hand to him. Stunned at her audacity, incredulous that Andy could suspect nothing, Ben glanced down at it, wondering how he could take it.

"I—I...Yeah, nice to see you again. I'm really happy you could join us on this trip. Look, I'm sorry, you'll have to excuse me. Jilly is—there was something I need to tell her—"

Ignoring the puzzled looks on their faces, Ben turned and made a run for the door—

And bumped right into Tess/Bess, coming out of the suite's kitchen with a tray of coffee mugs, one of which spilled onto Ben.

If he needed an excuse to leave, a wet spot on the crotch of his pants was as good as any.

CHAPTER 18

Discretion.

If that didn't work, spin.

And as a last attempt at triage, there was damage control.

Ben could have kept his mouth shut until they got back to D.C. In fact, he should have let it go, right then and there, take some time to collect his thoughts on how to position Abby's affair to Andy—

Well, to Abby first, since he was going to insist that she break the news to her husband.

He wasn't going to be a victim of "shoot the messenger." No way in hell.

Particularly since Andy's military experience ensured he was a crack shot.

But Abby's lover was right there at the fundraising dinner, too—front and center. Worse yet, she'd had him seated at the Mansfields' table, to her left, in fact. Lover boy wasn't overly attentive to her, just polite and reserved.

Too damn blatant. The sheer gall of it all.

And yet, Ben was willing to ignore it—

Until they both slipped away nonchalantly, first one then the other, at the beginning of Andy's speech.

Ben had to follow.

He gave them a five-minute head start, then took the elevator up to their floor. The desk clerk had never taken back the wrong electronic key. He put it in the lock and opened the door silently, and slipped down the hall to Abby and Andy's bedroom.

They had their backs to him, but were standing close together. Abby had changed into a kimono, flimsy and silky.

They hadn't heard him enter.

In time, though, she sensed his presence and turned toward him. She was startled to see someone standing there, but upon recognizing him, she smiled quizzically and held out her hand again.

That shocked him. How could she be so brazen, so outrageously heartless?

"Abby, what—what the hell do you think you're doing?" Ben growled.

The man turned now. His eyes searched Ben's face for some recognition. "Excuse me, but...Abby do you know this man?"

Ben scowled. "Bud, if I were you, I'd get lost, and fast."

The man stiffened. He glanced at Abby for some signal. Slowly she nodded. He picked up his briefcase and left the room.

Her eyes narrowed with confusion. "I'm sorry, I don't know what you—"

The quick strides that brought him to her side were driven by the anger surging inside of him. He watched her face lose its innocence, grow wary. "I'm asking you why you felt the need to do this to Andy."

Shock crossed her face. "Do what? What exactly do you think happened here?"

Seeing the shock and fear in her eyes made Ben sad—and angrier. "You tell me. What were you doing with that guy in your room just now—and earlier this afternoon?"

Abby turned white. "How did you know that?"

"Because I saw you together. And you were undressed! Just like you are now—"

Abigail fell back against the bed. She held one hand over her mouth. "Are you some kind of lunatic? What were you doing in my room earlier? What are you doing here now? How dare you accuse me of...Just what are you accusing me of, anyway?"

"Screwing around on Andy, for starters. Just admit it! Jesus, Abby, why talk him into running if you're just going to ruin it for him, anyway?"

"*Me—ruin* him?" She was laughing—no *crying*.

Was she having a nervous breakdown?

Enraged, she wrenched her wrist from his hand and stumbled across the room. Then rummaging through her purse, she pulled out a card and tossed it at his feet.

Ben picked it up:

Carl Torrance, M.D. - OB/GYN

Infertility Specialist, George Washington University

Jesus, I'm such an ass.

She opened her kimono and pointed down to her belly. "See this—these holes? They're from my infertility injections. That man is my *doctor*, Mr. Brinker. He did me the favor of meeting me here in Chicago, so that we could continue my treatments. Otherwise, I'd be back at square one by the time we got back to Washington. You see, I have to be poked like some masochistic human pincushion, every four hours in fact. *That's* what I do—for Andy. Because for ten years now, we've been trying to get pregnant. He wants a child so badly." A tear rolled down her cheek. "And so do I."

Ben opened his mouth to apologize but her furious stare stopped him dead in his tracks.

"The way I see it, Mr. Brinker, we can handle this one of two ways: First, I can tell my husband and, depending what I say, you may or may not have a job tomorrow." Seeing the color drain out of his face, she paused. "Or, I can take into account the fact that everything you said and did tonight was based on your fierce loyalty to the senator, and say nothing to him." She smiled, but there was no joy in her eyes. "Rest assured, Ben: no one loves Andy more than me. He knows it, and I know it. In the scheme of things, that's all that counts. And now that you know it, too, I hope you never forget it."

Her hands shook as she stooped to pick up her glasses where they'd fallen on the floor by the bed. "Oh, and by the way, please be kind enough to honor my secret. If Andy knew what I was going through, he'd insist I stop, and I have no intention of doing so. We both need this child. More than you'll ever know."

Her head high, she tied the kimono tightly around her waist and smoothed her mussed hair back into its chignon as she slammed the bathroom door behind her.

CHAPTER 19

Dirty tricks.

Ben had been a toddler during Watergate, so he hadn't lived through it, per se. Still, he had written his graduate thesis on the watershed event, so he had a thorough if academic understanding of its importance, politically, culturally, and legally.

But studying it was one thing. Running up against it from Talbot's organization was a master class.

Forget stretching the truth. All day, every day, both Talbot and his renowned political endorsers peppered the on-air pundits with innuendos, misstatements, distortions and outright lies about Andy Mansfield's voting record and policy positions. And to reinforce them, fake blogs were set up, ostensibly manned by a battery of anonymous Joe-the-Bloggers. But when the wife of one of the bloggers discovered his iChats to four online girlfriends, she spilled the beans to the Associated Press in a tell-all email, forwarding the TalbotForPresident.com how-to handbook, along with a few of the campaign's top secret emails espousing that day's talking points.

That antic was certainly nothing compared to the sinister dread of discovering that hackers—make that *Talbot's* hackers— had cracked the Mansfield campaign's computer server.

The first inkling Ben had of this was when he logged onto MansfieldForPresident.com on a dreary February morning, and was instantaneously rerouted to a porn site called LollypopLove.com (along with two-hundred-thousand other viewers, he was to learn later).

Immediately he called over to the campaign's website management firm, the Conover Group, to ask what the fuck was happening. They assured him that their IT security people were already on it. Unfortunately, that naughty prank wasn't the worst of it. Moments later Sukie burst into his office, frantic with the news, confirmed by Conover, that the hackers had also previewed some of Mansfield's upcoming video ads, and had stolen the master email address list of Mansfield supporters.

They'd even hacked into Andy's Twitter account and texted lewd comments to his female constituents, suggesting they hook up with him "the next time I roll into town."

Sukie was thunderstruck. "Oh my God! Now some 80,000 women think he's a Weiner-esque man-ho!"

A cold chill ran through Ben's veins as he dialed Fred's secure cell number. It was immediately obvious to him that Fred wasn't at CIA Headquarters when he heard some chirpy voice in the background call out, "Can I take your order?"

Of course Fred was already clued into both situations. His first comment was that the vile sex act being performed on the new Mansfield welcome page was something he'd never experienced, but had been privy to once while on a surveillance mission in Bangkok.

"That's city's name is no malapropism, all things considered," he said, between bites of something much too greasy for seven o'clock in the morning.

Ben was in no mood for any jokes. "Is that all you have to say on the matter?"

After a gulp and a sigh, Fred responded with just one word: "Digits."

Then he hung up.

A half-hour later there was a single, loud knock on the door. Standing in front of Ben was a skinny olive-skinned kid with a large curly afro. He could not have been more than sixteen years old. The kid handed him a card. On it was written one word: *DIGITS*.

Before Ben could say a word, the kid put his finger to his lips, indicating that Ben should keep his mouth shut. Then he opened the computer bag he was holding and pulled out a laptop.

Whatever software program he clicked onto created what looked like a 3-D architect's rendering of the office. Several hot spots lit up on the computer-generated image. Pulling out a cell phone, Digits walked over to where the spots were indicated, then pointed the phone at the location while tapping out a series of numbers. When he was done, he sat back down at the computer and started hacking away. "Okay, we're clear. Got any java in this joint?"

Ben nodded, and moved toward the coffeemaker. "Don't tell me you work with Fred."

"Don't worry, I won't." The kid didn't even look up when he answered, but tapped the keyboard while scanning the sequence of numbers that filled his screen. Ben noticed he had just a bit of a Spanish accent, more Caribbean than, say, Mexican. Perhaps Puerto Rican? It was too slight to place.

"By that I mean, you look too young to be at Langley."

Digits stopped typing and smirked. "Shit, dude, you gotta be kidding! Langley is the very *last* place I'd work."

"Why is that?"

"Because those bastards killed my pop." The kid shrugged. "At one of their black sites. They call it Hotel Transylvania. Outside of Bucharest. He had the unfortunate luck of being one of their 'guests'."

"How do you know all this?"

"Because I hacked into their computers and saw his file."

Ben blinked hard. If this kid was smart enough to do that, well then hell yeah, he wanted Digits on their side. "Do you mind telling me—what was his crime?"

Digits's fingers roamed the keyboard, but he didn't look up. "He tried to assassinate Manolo Padilla."

"No shit!" Ben sat down hard. "The Venezuelan president?"

"Yeah, their little puppet." The kid nodded, and started typing again. "Want to hear something funny? If he tried to do it today, well hell, he'd get some kind of damn Medal of Honor from those bastards!...Wait—"

He typed in one last backspace, then nodded toward the computer's screen. "There, your site is secure again. I'll have your network's server cleared up within the hour. Fred says that the Talbot campaign is claiming that they've been hacked too, but I agree with him: that's just some CYA bullshit. They just want to throw some stank on the Dems. But here's the beauty part: as payback, I created a file they won't be able to resist. It's labeled 'VIP Donors', but it's really a Trojan dropper."

"What the hell is that?"

"A super-virus that corrupts the hacker's system. It will also search their server for any Ghost Squad activity. Whatever it finds will be forwarded to one of Fred's email accounts, and archived in a secure cloud that only he and I can access."

Ben shook his head in awe. "Jesus...So, how did Fred find you?"

"He didn't. I found *him*." The kid looked up again. "When I hacked into my father's file, it included a report from Fred. He'd been observing my dad's key interrogator, some sadist named Smith. Something my dad said made Fred realize that Pop wasn't the attempted assassin. He tried hard to override Smith, to get my father released. Unfortunately the asshole who was running the agency denied the request. Not that it mattered. By the time it made it to his desk, Smith had killed my father. They claimed it was a suicide."

"What did your father do in civilian life?"

"He was a CFO for Dia Petróleo, the Venezuelan subsidiary of Sundial Oil." Digits shrugged. "Wouldn't hurt a flea, but knew where the bodies were buried. And the money, too."

"How long ago was this?"

"*Eleven years ago.* Padilla had only been dictator for a year."

Eleven years ago. At that point in time, Ben realized, Clemson Talbot was CIA director.

It was too much of a coincidence.

CHAPTER 20

"He's got them on the run, and everyone knows it!" In her excitement Abby clenched Ben's hand so hard that her wedding ring struck a nerve in his palm.

He winced but didn't let go. Heck, why would he? Every time she touched him, he imagined it was Maddy.

It was late March. They were standing in the back of the Air Force One Pavilion at the Ronald Reagan Presidential Library, watching as Andy, Clemson Talbot, and the only other Republican in the race—the evangelicals' candidate of choice, Congressman Clyde Dooley—debated each other in the first of a series of multi-candidate appearances sponsored by the Republican National Committee. Political pundits had already pronounced it Talbot's to lose, whereas Andy only had to reiterate the key points of his platform to come out the victor.

He was doing that with his usual charismatic ease. "Vice President Talbot wants to placate America with half-truths and fear. Why not just the facts, Mr. Vice President?"

He played to the camera, which zoomed in on his handsome, square-jawed face. "Here's one very important fact: Our government now wastes 35 billion dollars on subsidies to the oil industry—an industry in which one company alone, Exxon Mobil Corporation, earned 9.92 billion dollars in profits, in over just three months. Here's another fact, Mr. Vice President: That amount would cover all Social Security benefit payments for a full ninety days. Fact Three: It would also pay for Ivy League educations for some 60,000 students." His hand swept toward the audience. "I'm sure the Morrisons—that nice couple from Milwaukee, sitting there in the front row—would appreciate seeing the tuition covered for their seventeen-year-old son, Jeff—"

Ben was just as excited as Abby, but he couldn't pass up the opportunity to tease her just a little about her adoration for her husband. "That's why they say love is blind, Abby. Though, I'll admit, it does seem he's won this thing hands down. Talbot looks green around the gills."

Abby's laugh was deep and sweet. Surprised at being so unguarded, she finally let go of his hand in order to cover her face in mock shame.

Damn, if only I'd kept my mouth shut, he thought. He rubbed his thumb over the spot on his palm indented by her ring, not because it hurt but because it proved how far they'd come together in such a few short months. Since the day she took him into her confidence about the infertility drugs, both had come to understand and appreciate their respective roles in Andy's life.

Abby was keenly aware of Ben's contribution to the campaign. He had an innate genius for correctly guessing Talbot's next moves, and he zealously safeguarded the senator's All-American persona to the media. But it was his tireless enthusiasm in front of the campaign's staff that inspired her to cast off her shyness, to make herself readily available for any event they deemed necessary for her to attend.

And realizing that she might otherwise have used that precious time to address her infertility problem, Ben's appreciation for her increased tenfold, too—although it was plain to anyone near them how much she and Andy enjoyed the time they spent together on the road. On the campaign's plane, they snuggled and held hands.

It helped, too, that Abby never played the diva. Nor did she complain about some unimportant slight, or offer an opinion—that is, unless she was asked for one.

Over the next four months, Ben found himself asking her quite often. In fact it surprised him how completely he came to trust her innate instincts about Andy's constituents; and more importantly, about Andy's mood.

Without doubt, Abigail Vandergalen Mansfield was proving to be a seasoned road warrior and a team player.

Ben wished that Maddy was also there at his side, instead of thousands of miles away, doing who knows what. Maybe with the Invisible Man...He tried not to think about that.

And yet, standing so close to Abby, Ben couldn't help but compare her to Maddy. One was gracious and accommodating, while the other was a tempestuous wild child. Not just physically, but emotionally too, they were different as night and day...

"—coming around. Don't you agree?"

Abby's worried tone pierced his guilty fantasy like a bubble. "I'm sorry, I was daydreaming. What were you asking?"

"I was commenting on some of the GOP's deep pockets. Like Rosalyn and Collin Davenport. They're old friends of the family...well, *my* family. Do you recall a contribution from them as of yet?"

Ben shook his head. "No. But you know Andy. He can be both stubborn and cocky, particularly when he has a chance to tweak the noses of the old boys' club. Of course we knew we'd make some enemies along the way, but I'd still like to keep a few of the party's bigger donors as our friends. We're coming up to another fundraising deadline, and things are tight."

"Let me see what I can do," she murmured.

Within a week's time, Andy's off-the-cuff comments were less caustic regarding his own party, and Abby was hosting some private teas at their Georgetown townhouse with some very influential wives, including Rosalyn Davenport.

Before the end of the month, the Davenports sent in two checks for $250,000 each.

CHAPTER 21

The paid agitators sent to the Tampa "Andrew Mansfield for President" rally by Talbot's handlers were kids in their twenties: actors, really, not the fresh-faced college kids they were pretending to be. They carried placards with anti-war slogans, and their chants—hollered at the top of their lungs—accused Mansfield of being a warmonger. The worst kind at that—one who'd bombed innocent civilians from the safety of his fighter jet.

Instead of having his security detail throw them out before some of the hotheaded vets in the audience could beat them bloody for disrespecting country and flag, Mansfield invited them onto the stage with him.

Scripted chants were one thing; improv against one of the Senate's best extemporaneous orators was another. The faux protesters knew they were out of their element. Thrown into the spotlight with Mansfield, they listened, slack-jawed, as he described the depth of his loss after the untimely death of his parents; the fellowship and sense of purpose he found in the Marine Corps; and yes the horrors of war, even as seen from the cockpit of an F-4S. "Great nations, those with the will and the might, must use it sparingly. Only when attacked. And never to claim the natural resources of another country."

It was the perfect segue into Mansfield's speech on 100 percent energy independence. His eyes never once wavered from the protesters as he talked.

Afterward, when buttonholed by an NBC reporter, one of the agitators proclaimed he was voting for Mansfield. Another said he was joining the Marines.

Talbot fired his Florida state campaign manager that night.

CHAPTER 22

By June Maddy no longer left before dawn, but lingered in Ben's bed with him.

On the few Sundays he found himself in town, she allowed him to make her breakfast in bed. Then they'd share the *Washington Post* while lounging out on his postage stamp-sized deck for an hour or two, before she disappeared again—for a night, or a day, or a week.

He soon learned not to count the many days they were apart, but to appreciate the precious hours they spent together.

Then in July, something changed. She showed up at his place with a sack of groceries and proceeded to make him the most delicious overcooked spaghetti he'd ever eaten. He was well aware that they had finally turned a corner.

In August, when she wrote down her cell phone number for him and stuck it on his fridge under a *Mansfield for President* magnet, he realized they were finally a real couple.

That's when he suggested she join Abby, the senator and him on one of their many out-of-town campaign trips.

Because it was Maddy he was asking, he knew he was going out on a limb to even suggest it. Still, he wasn't prepared for her reaction. The way she laughed at him—raucously, incredulously—rubbed against the rawest spot on his ego.

"What's so funny?"

"I don't know. I just assumed there were enough campaign groupies out there already." She busied herself with the *Post's* crossword puzzle. "I'd hate to cramp anyone's style."

"Yeah, sure, I turn a head or two, but you know I'm a true blue guy." It was the truth. If he were a horn dog, if he weren't so head over heels in love with her, there were plenty of opportunities for one-night stands. "And you're no groupie, you're my girlfriend. Only you won't let anyone know that."

"You're wrong, Ben. I'm not your girlfriend. You're *my* lover. And no one else knows that because that's the way we both want it." She busied herself with the puzzle's 42 Down. "What brought this on, all of a sudden?"

"Just something Andy said. I guess that...Well, sometimes I wouldn't mind having what Andy and Abby have."

Her sly smile hardened into a grimace. "Oh yeah? And what is that, pray tell?"

He swallowed hard. Obviously he'd hit a nerve. "They're—or at least they seem to be soul mates."

"Looks can be deceiving."

"It's not just how they look, or act, together. It's the way he talks about her."

Nonchalantly she wrote in 14 Across. "Oh yeah? What exactly does he say?"

Fuck it. In for a dime, in for a dollar. "That she keeps him on the straight and narrow. That he's running because of her. That she's his angel."

"His angel, eh? How very sweet."

There was edge to her voice, but he didn't care. In fact, it egged him on, to make his case. "It's not just that. Look at all she's going through for him—"

"What exactly do you mean by that?"

"All the infertility shots! You know..." But it was obvious by the look on her face that she didn't. "Shit! I just assumed that she and you—well, never mind. Damn. She certainly knows how to keep a secret."

"I'm glad one of you does." The topic must have been boring her, because she went back to her puzzle. "I wonder what Andy thinks of all that."

"He doesn't know. She hasn't told him." Ben wanted to add, *Those are the kind of sacrifices you make when you're in love.* Instead, he kept his mouth shut. "But if he found out, I imagine he'd be ecstatic."

Personally, and politically. A pregnancy would be another plus for the campaign. Besides making for great press, it would reaffirm the senator's youthfulness, as opposed to Talbot's. Hey, it worked for John and Jackie, right?

She shrugged. "Well Ben, I won't tell him, if you don't. Out of respect for my sister. But as to whether or not I'll be your Abby, forget about it. I'm no angel. And whatever you presume they have isn't what I want to have with you. I like things just the way they are." She turned back to her puzzle. "But I'll tell you what: I'll give serious consideration about taking our relationship public."

"Sounds good to me. But why the change of heart?"

"I guess I'm tired of the way things are. It's time to shake things up."

I hear you.

CHAPTER 23

A week later Maddy showed up at a Mansfield campaign rally, in Annapolis. "To support Abby" is how she put it, but in fact, Abby had been detained at a radio interview in Baltimore. That was okay. Mansfield was on fire, the crowd was stoked, and both Maddy and Ben were high on the vibe. So high that when Mansfield finished his speech and the crowd gave him a standing ovation, Ben absently kissed Maddy—

And she didn't pull away.

Until they both realized that Abby was staring at them.

Slowly she started toward them. But then something, or someone, caught her attention. She looked as if she'd seen a ghost standing behind them.

Ben turned around to see Andy glad-handing his way through the dense mob that enveloped him. The senator hadn't seen them yet. Abby must've realized that too. Stiffly she nodded, but turned and threaded her way through the crowd until she was at her husband's side, nudging him, oh so subtly, in the opposite direction.

Ben looked at Maddy. "What the hell just happened?"

Maddy didn't seem at all shocked by Abby's reaction. "Poor Ben! I guess our little family reunion didn't go exactly the way you pictured it...Hey, don't be so sad! Wow, I do believe you'll truly miss me."

Abby's summons came the next day: a handwritten invitation for brunch the following Sunday.

Quite pointedly, she requested that he come alone.

He would not have shown it to Maddy, but she'd arrived at his apartment before him. Having scooped up the mail that had fallen through the front door slot, of course she recognized her sister's handwriting.

But unlike Ben, she was not convinced that Abby's anger would blow over.

That didn't faze him. "Even if it doesn't, what does it matter? She doesn't have a say as to whom I see. Or whom you see, either, for that matter."

"You've said it yourself: He listens to her. So, if you don't drop me, you'll be out of a job." Maddy shrugged. "Ben, every family has its black sheep. In ours, I'm it. Believe me, I knew this day would come for us. Let's just take our lumps and move on."

"Andy needs me just as much as I need him. And we respect each other. Andy will be happy for us. And he'll help Abby put it into perspective. You'll see."

She didn't say another word. Not that she had to. Her love play, fierce and tender both, said it all.

Afterward he didn't remember closing his eyes, but when he opened them again the room was filled with sunlight, his cell phone was buzzing, and Maddy, his sweet Maddy, was nowhere to be found.

He did find her note, however, which she'd left on her pillow:

Goodbye, Lancelot. —Maddy

What?...That's it? Hell no. *No way...*

The cell's buzz brought him to life. Was it Maddy? He grabbed it.

"Hi, Mr. Brinker, this is Tasha Sullivan with the *Washington Post*. Can you give me a quote on a story I'm doing about Senator Mansfield—"

"*What?*—No! I'm..." He couldn't even finish the sentence. He snapped the phone shut.

Blinded with anger, he hurled it at the wall.

Fuck Maddy. And fuck Abby, for ruining what I shared, finally, with Maddy.

When he calmed down enough to pick it up and open it, he was surprised to hear the reporter still on the other end. "Did I catch you at a bad time?" she asked hesitantly.

He sighed. "Nah. Couldn't be more perfect. So, what's up?"

CHAPTER 24

"Ah, Ben! Welcome!" Abigail Mansfield's false cheeriness barely hid the slight quiver in her voice.

She had rushed to answer the door as opposed to letting Andy get it. It was her one rule with Andy that, whenever he was not on the road, Sunday was to be their one day off. No one was in the house, not even the maid.

Andy's usual Sunday routine was to jog after church. That would have given her all the time she needed to read Ben the riot act and allow him to collect himself before Andy came home. But as it turned out, Andy had been on the phone with Sukie since the moment they returned from early morning services. She'd apologized for interrupting their Sunday, but had something urgent to tell him about some senate bill he was sponsoring. His being there when Ben showed up wasn't the ideal scenario, but Abby would have to make do.

No matter. Ben would see it her way, or else.

Civility dictated that Ben be smiling, that he should say something pleasant back to her, shake her extended hand warmly and sincerely. She was, after all, the wife of his employer. And besides, they'd become friends, too. At least, she'd thought so. Two road warriors fighting the same cause, protecting the same precious cargo:

The reputation of the future president of the United States.

But no. Ben's posture was stiff, his nod curt. He stared back at her with cold, cruel eyes. He didn't smile as much as bare his teeth, as if to dare her to try her best to change his mind.

About Maddy.

Abby was the enemy now. That much she knew.

All because of Maddy.

But Abby knew full well the extent of the emotional damage Maddy could cause. Maddy's disregard for her own reputation, her own safety, had been a sore subject between the sisters for some time now. No, it was up to her to make Ben Brinker aware of what his involvement with her careless, petulant sister could cost them. There could be no other alternative.

And if Ben wasn't smart enough to see her point, she'd have no choice but to ask Andy to dismiss him immediately. It would mortify her to bring it up to him—

But she'd have to, because there was too much at stake.

Well, enough already. I refuse to let her sully Andy, too. To let her ruin all our lives.

Abby led Ben into the living room, watching out of the corner of her eye as he took in every detail of its décor: the expensive antiques, their formality offset by a couple of shabby chic settees; the deep molding surrounding the tray ceiling; and the coffee urn and the glass pitcher of orange juice that shared a silver tray on the coffee table with Wedgwood cups and saucers and three beveled tumblers.

Built-in bookshelves shared the walls with formal paintings that were both expensive and original. Ben lingered over one, a winter landscape by William Sidney Mount.

So he has good taste. Well, that's a step up from Maddy's previous lovers, thought Abby. Who was it last time? The Hell's Angel? No wait, that Neanderthal was several boyfriends ago. Her most recent breakup had been with the rabid *Mother*

Jones reporter. Or was it the sadistic Russian diplomat?

Somewhere among all these losers had been the quote-unquote art consultant who was fronting the mob's cocaine distribution to primarily well-heeled Washington party animals. Uncle Preston's way of dealing with that potential media scandal was to become the majority stockholder in the tabloid newspaper about to break that juicy little story.

Maddy's response was to laugh when she heard about it. "Deduct the stock from my inheritance," was her blithe response to him.

Uncle Preston was right: Maddy's tarnish was something the Alcott and Vandergalen names—let alone her brother-in-law's presidential campaign—could ill afford, and he was under the assumption he'd made that quite clear to her.

Apparently he hadn't. Well, Abby was going to spell it out to Ben. Maddy's shenanigans were the last thing Andy—or his campaign manager—needed.

"—I think we can get Collins Snowe and Ayotte Spencer to co-sponsor. And since we want bi-partisan ownership, put out feelers to Barbara Boxer and Al Franken—" Andy's voice floated out to them from the adjoining room, the Mansfields' library.

Abby shrugged apologetically. "Sorry about that. The Veterans's Benefits bill. He may be on the phone for a while." She pointed to the pitcher. "Andy likes mimosas. Will you join me in having one?"

"Sure, why not?" Ben didn't even bother turning around when he answered.

His casual tone irritated her. Couldn't he sense the turmoil he'd caused her?

Well, that's par for the course, for someone who's dating Maddy.

Only when Abby handed him a tumbler of the spiked juice did

he turn toward her to give her a dismissive nod before plopping himself down casually onto her favorite Duncan Phyfe settee.

But he said nothing at all.

As if daring her to speak first.

You son of a bitch.

With as much control as she could muster, she set her face into a smile. "So, this thing—this 'relationship' you have with Maddy: Is it serious?"

"Yeah. I love her. She's the one." He said it so matter-of-factly that it broke her heart.

"Ah, I see." She took a deep breath. "I'd like to ask you a favor. I'd—I'd like to ask you to leave her alone."

"I don't understand."

"You'll just have to take my word for it that it won't work out. Not for you, anyway."

"With all due respect, I don't think that's up to you to say. It's between Maddy and me." Seeing her look of disbelief, he paused. "Listen, Abby, I can just imagine what you're thinking: that I'm not good enough for your sister—"

"No! No—that's not it at all." Her anxiety came out in staccato stutters. "Ben, it's not you. It's Maddy. She's—well, she's trouble." She sighed as she closed her eyes.

"Granted, yeah, Maddy's a handful. Obviously she's been a bit wild in the past. I'm guessing she went through a couple of rough relationships. Something you've obviously been spared. But—"

"*A handful?* No, you don't understand! She's done this before, this little game. Trust me, Ben, I'm telling you that—that *you don't mean anything to her.*" The words stuck in her throat. "As for me being 'spared,' how dare you presume—"

She stopped short, perhaps because she was revealing too much; or perhaps because of the pitying look on Ben's face.

Then, as a final plea: "Ben, please believe me: this could cause

Andy a great deal of—"

"Abby, get real! What does Maddy's relationship with me have to do with Andy? We're all grown-ups here. We've all made mistakes. But we can't live in the past." Ben shook his head adamantly. "Hell, I thought that you of all people would be happy for us."

Her stomach twisted into a large, hard knot. To stifle the urge to slap the snide smirk off his face, she picked up the heavy pitcher again to pour a glass for herself, but she was so angry that her hand trembled, and the pitcher tilted precariously.

Instinctively Ben put his hand over hers. But instead of steadying her, his touch had the opposite effect. The heat from his strong thick fingers shocked her so.

Without thinking, she turned her hand at an angle and the juice cascaded out of the glass and into one of the teacups.

Mortified, Abby mumbled an apology as she frantically sopped up the mess with one of the napkins. But instead of moving his hand away, he grasped hers even tighter. She couldn't fight the urge to look into his eyes:

His sad, sad eyes.

Did he find her pathetic?

No...He was looking at her as if she were the most beautiful woman in the world.

The thought of that look—of what it meant for Maddy—made her blush deeply.

But what about Maddy? She still had to deal with the problem of her sister.

"I'm...so...sorry," Ben murmured.

She looked up, stunned.

He gets it.

"Oh...You do understand!" Relief flooded her face. Then pretending to be caught up in the task of cleaning up the spill, she said as casually as she could muster, "Ben, what you're feeling—it's not easy, and I appreciate that. But in the long run, it could never be." She paused, but had to add: "You really do understand now, don't you?"

Ben paused for what seemed like forever. "Yes," he said finally. "It's over."

Thank you, God.

When she looked up again, she was smiling. She made some silly joke about being clumsy and thanked him again for his help. But sensing this wasn't enough to show her appreciation, she proffered another olive branch, in the form of a compliment: How Andy was so impressed with Ben's drive, his determination—

Suddenly Andy was there at her side, smothering her in a bear hug and a kiss, slapping Ben on the back, asking what he had missed and calling them both "the two most important people in my life."

She wondered if Andy's remark had embarrassed Ben as much as it had embarrassed her.

Yes, it had. She knew because he almost went white at the compliment.

Ben had been feigning interest in some ugly painting when Abby asked him, very casually, to give up the woman he loved.

Her request, coming out of the blue, stunned him. Hey, sure, he knew the sisters weren't close at all. Still, he thought he could chide Abby for being so small-minded, that he could convince her that he and Maddy were the real thing, just like her and Andy.

That Maddy deserved her own chance at true love.

Why would Abby deny her sister a shot at happiness? For the sake of propriety?

One sister didn't deserve to have it all. Certainly not at the expense of the other.

He felt great reading her the riot act. And yeah, he got his jollies when he realized he had rattled her. He was still laying into her when she handed him his glass with a trembling hand—

And that's when she spilled the pitcher.

The moment he touched her hand, he regretted it. The current that surged between them was like nothing he'd ever felt.

Not even with Maddy.

Damn it, what the hell is happening to me?

It must have affected her, too, because she was shakier than ever. She looked as if she was about to burst into tears. And her words were coming out all jumbled...

Before he could stop himself, the words had tumbled out: "I'm...so sorry."

She looked up at him. A hopeful smile quivered on her lips.

He lost himself in her beautiful face. Those sharply cut cheekbones, the gentle arch of her brows, those luminous blue eyes, shaped *exactly* like Maddy's—

And yet she was so different. Missing was that keen edginess that elevated his heart every time he saw Maddy, the calculating shrewdness that lurked behind those eyes, promising him the time of his life.

But in its place was something just as heart-wrenching: a haunting vulnerability.

Abby blushed so deeply that he wondered, Does she know what I'm thinking?

He felt guilty for this obvious attraction. As if he was betraying Maddy...

Abby didn't look at him, thank God for that. She was too busy cleaning up the mess. But his words put color in her cheeks, and a smile, albeit a shaky one, on those sweet lips.

Otherwise she would have seen the pain in his eyes when she exclaimed: "Oh...You do understand! Ben, what you're feeling—it's not easy, and I appreciate that. But in the long run, you'll see that it could never be." She said it as if it were a foregone conclusion. "You really do understand now, don't you?"

Right then and there, he realized that any other answer would be unfathomable to her.

"Yes," he had finally muttered. "It's over."

Relief flooded her face. Laughter tumbled out of her along with a tender compliment for all that he was doing for Andy—

She thinks I've ended the affair because I'm afraid of compromising my job with Andy. Well, fuck it, she can believe whatever she wants. But I can't tell her the truth: I can't give up Maddy. If I have to buy time between now and the election, so be it.

Afterward, Maddy and I can do whatever we want.

They were both glad when Andy bounded into the room, slapping Ben on the back before giving Abby a hug and a sweet kiss on the forehead.

"Hope I haven't missed much," he said, pouring himself a glass from the pitcher.

If only you knew, they both thought.

CHAPTER 25

The address Kenny Lafferty dug up for him was a funky loft residence in Washington's Morgan Adams neighborhood, just up the block from DuPont Circle. Ben arrived around dusk. The front door was locked, but it only took him a minute to find the key where it was hidden: over the doorsill, where he put his spare, too.

The ground floor was a studio. Sculptures were scattered throughout, in various phases of completion. Most were tall, sharp and angular, and reached to the heavens seen through the skylight that made up the loft's ceiling, their sharp spears piercing, foreboding.

Just like Maddy.

At first he didn't see her there, on the balcony, staring down at him. When he finally noticed her, the sight of her took his breath away. Not because she was naked beneath her short sheer silk robe, or because she was so beautiful, but because the haunted look in her eyes reminded him so much of Abby.

The robe fell open when she beckoned him up, casually, as if she'd been expecting him all along.

As if she knew he'd choose her, no matter what.

He ran up the stairs two steps at a time.

"What did you say to her?"

Above Maddy's bed the skylight revealed a dark sky pocked with tiny, glittering stars.

It must have been after midnight. They'd quit making love an hour or so ago. Both of them should have been exhausted, should have fallen dead asleep. But she, like he, was staring up into space. And he was happy to see that she, too, had a smile on her face.

I could lay here like this with you for the rest of my life.

"I lied. I told her it was over between us."

Maddy propped herself up onto her side. "Ben, you now understand, don't you? Why Abby can't know about us?"

He nodded, resigned. "Until after the election, at least."

"Yes, exactly. Because after that, it won't matter. Not even to Abby."

Eventually she drifted off to sleep in his arms. He watched as she snored softly, but her sleep was not tranquil. Her brows arched in consternation, and her eyelids flickered as she battled some demon in her sleep.

Whatever it is, my love, I'll never let it hurt you.

CHAPTER 26

"Andy's not going to win. It's as simple as that."

Paul's prediction, given so matter-of-factly between bites of his aged medium rare filet mignon, almost caused Ben to choke on his own lunch entree, a teriyaki-grilled wild salmon.

Before Ben had a chance to respond, Paul continued: "And we should save him from the biggest mistake of his career—of his *life*—before it's too late."

If the two men had been anywhere else but the Taft Room of the exclusive and private University Club, Ben probably would have shouted, "What the fuck are you saying?"

Or more likely, he would have yanked Paul up by the lapels of his gray pinstriped double worsted Anderson & Sheppard suit and slammed him against the wall.

Instead he swallowed the hunk of wild Coho stuck in his throat and took a slow sip of water from the beveled crystal goblet in front of him. Only when he was sure he could talk without cursing a blue streak did he open his mouth. "You're kidding, right? Or on acid? Because I know you're aware that our guy is right on Talbot's tail—"

Here it was, the middle of September, and Andy was on fire—in the polls, in the media, and on the senate floor.

It was a full four months before the first primary, and Andy's campaign war chest was almost as full as Talbot's. Better yet, while most of Talbot's donations were at the legal campaign limit, Andy's were in smaller increments, coming from a much broader base of constituents. Four times as many donors had given online, too, which was proof of Andy's ability to reach voters who were willing to use their money to back candidates they believed in.

Ben just assumed that Paul's invitation to the club was to celebrate this great news.

No wonder he asked me to keep this little meeting on the QT. He's Andy's best friend, for Chrissakes!

The table Paul had reserved for them was in a private alcove, and the hostess's route had taken them past several of the Capitol's biggest powerbrokers. Ben recognized all their faces, but Paul knew more of them personally. Or at least, they knew him well enough to call him over and pump his hand.

As their sumptuous courses were being delivered on silver platters by the club's discreet butlers, Paul engaged Ben in small talk: the latest gossip raging through D.C.'s tony social set, and GOP insider buzz that wasn't within hearing distance of Ben's own informants. No, Ben's contacts dwelled too far below the rarefied air inhabited by Paul, Andy, and their ilk—

He suddenly realized why Paul had insisted that they meet here.

Why, you sonofabitch! You want to intimidate me so I pull out of Andy's campaign—

Or sabotage it.

"I know I sound like some kind of asshole, or traitor, to even suggest that. But it's time to face facts. Look, let me level with you." Paul leaned forward, though it wasn't necessary. The drone of conversation in the room beyond, coupled with the clink of polished silver to glistening china, was drowning out his traitorous offensive. "The guys who have supported Andy from the beginning—these guys who have *made* Andy—feel he's jumping the gun. *It's just not his time.* He's still green. Another term in the

Senate will season him, rid him of that idealism that seems to get him so far off course. He might even be tapped as the vice presidential nominee—"

"Well they're wrong. Andy is the real thing, and it looks like the public knows it, too. And that's the one thing that the power brokers can't control.

"You'd be surprised by what they can—and *do*—control." Paul looked around uneasily. "Unfortunately, Andy is making a lot of powerful enemies. He thinks he can stand between them and what they feel—what they *know*—is their legacies. Well, he can't. Ben, trust me, these men will stop at nothing to control the outcome of this race." He paused and took a gulp of his wine. "That's where you come in. Look, everyone recognizes the role you've played these past few months to put our man on top. In the future, should you make a few miscalculations—say, in the directions you give either Eddie or Spike—or if you let a few of the senior staffers go and replace them with volunteers...Well, you know how fast things can go downhill from there."

Ben sat in a stony silence while Paul twitched uncomfortably in his brocade Queen Anne wingback. Finally Paul murmured, "They realize that there is a price for such...an act."

Yeah okay, now we get down to brass tacks. "How much?"

"Quadruple your rate. And—and the party's presidential frontrunner, from here on out."

All that, just for selling out Andy Mansfield.

The one candidate who could ruin Talbot's chances for the presidency.

Ben let that sink in. No doubt about it, the money was tempting. But the brass ring was another twenty years of elections. He, too, would have a legacy, recorded in history books.

His name, right there next to *their* chosen few.

What had Digits called Padilla? Oh yeah, a *puppet*.

Now they wanted him to be their puppet, too.

Ben patted his mouth with his napkin. When he was done, he looked Paul right in the eye.

"Forget it. Ain't happening. But thanks for lunch." He stood up to leave. "Oh, and by the way, don't doubt that I will be telling Andy about this little conversation."

Paul turned white. For a second a fog enveloped his eyes. Finally he closed them, fatigue and failure heavy on his lids. "Yeah, okay. Your integrity in regard to your client is duly noted. To be honest with you, it was only out of concern for Abby that I'm asking." Paul's eyes softened as he spoke of her. "You know, I introduced the two of them. I was the best man at their wedding. And I—I dated her before he did. I only wished she had fallen for me instead."

"Seems to me she made the right choice. It's always nice when your spouse can stand on his own two feet. But to do that, you need a spine."

Ben's insult hit its mark. He could tell by the way Paul sat upright.

Frowning, Paul signaled for the check. "She's known these people all of her life. She grew up with them. But if he continues on this path, they'll drop her and never look back. She'll have to go back with him to his daddy's pig farm and learn to love it."

If that's your Hail Mary play, it sucks. It's a piss poor reason to sell out your friend.

"Your loyalty to Abby is touching, Paul. When this is all over and Abby is First Lady, I'm sure you'll get an invitation to the Lincoln bedroom. As will the rest of her loyal friends. So tell them to hang in there. It'll be worth the wait."

Ben walked away without a backward glance.

CHAPTER 27

"You've fucked up. Again."

No hello, what's happening, lay it on me, nothing. Smith hadn't expected warm fuzzies from Talbot, but the least the bastard could do was hear him out.

Since the Jorge Leon debacle, Ghost Squad activities in Venezuela had been unsuccessful at best, and fatal at worst. Padilla's personal chef sacrificed his beloved *abuela* rather than poison the leader's favorite dessert: *arroz con leche.* And the operative who threatened to expose one of Padilla's generals as a bathhouse regular in Caracas's gay underground had been found in a trunk, chopped up into little pieces. Attached to a forlorn middle finger was a note that read *"Cochinos gringos, coño e madre!"*

So yeah, no matter how much lipstick Smith slapped on that pig of an operation, bottom line was that he'd fucked it up, royally.

"The latest polls show Mansfield right on my heels, no thanks to your incompetence. Hell, your men couldn't even bug his campaign offices properly!"

Smith winced. It stuck in his craw that the electronic surveillance had somehow been stymied. "Didn't you say you have someone on the inside? What kind of recon are you getting?"

"It sucks. Hasn't been the intel windfall we were hoping for."

"Perhaps I should be handling the asset." It was a sore point with Smith that he wasn't being given full control of the mission.

"Why? So you can fuck that up, too?" Talbot ran his hand through his few thin hairs. "I'm surrounded by incompetents! In the meantime Mansfield's numbers—and his online donations—are through the damn roof! Everyone loves him: College kids, soccer moms, Joe Sixpacks. Hell, the Lipstick Lobby wants to date him."

Smith started to point out to Talbot that he still had the Evangelicals on his side, now that photos of Clyde Dooley's crossdressing had been leaked to the public, but he bit his tongue. Talbot wasn't in the mood for jokes. "Well then, that leaves the door open to innuendo. We can always rustle up an old girlfriend or two who'd be willing to vouch that he still sees her, on the sly. That would shred his credibility."

Talbot shifted his bulk uncomfortably. "It's not that easy. At least not in this case. The old men don't want another salacious Republican scandal. And time is getting short—"

For once Talbot was right about that. At this point, only a Hail Mary pass would do, but Talbot had already balked at the one thing that would put him over the top.

Bastard just didn't have the stomach for it.

Oh, well. Early retirement wouldn't be so bad. All of Smith's money was already offshore. All he had to do was find a warm, sandy beach somewhere, preferably topless—

"—How many times is it, now? You're becoming a liability. To everyone," Talbot hissed. "A vote was taken last night, and you don't want to know how close you came to...Well, never mind—"

Don't threaten me, you overstuffed bag of wind, Smith thought. I can crush your larynx with my thumb, and be in Bangkok before they find your bloated corpse in the Chesapeake—

"—happy to hear that I've reconsidered your previous proposal."

The palm trees faded against the new reality of the situation. "Come again?"

"I got the old men to agree to your Plan B."

Smith adjusted his rearview mirror carefully. "You're saying, you've gotten approval for the fake attack, here in the US?"

"What, do I have to draw you a picture?" Talbot smirked. "It's a go. But there are some preconditions."

"Such as?"

Talbot pulled a folded paper from his pocket. Smith glanced over the typed list.

"These cities have to be exempted. They are too important as business centers. And besides, the real estate is too expensive."

You mean, the old men have too many investments in them, Smith thought. He tried hard to keep a straight face. "You can rest easy. Even I can't envision Padilla invading Aspen."

Talbot's look of relief was evidence he missed the joke. No surprise there. "Great. So, what would be a viable target, in your opinion?"

"Las Vegas. On New Year's Eve. Big crowds, lots of news coverage already."

Talbot sniffed. "Works for me."

Smith had never doubted it. Downscale and fly-over. Filled with drunk tourists in polyester. And conventioneers. Nope, not Talbot's kind of town, at all.

Smith went in for the kill. "We only have ten weeks, so we have to work fast. It will require some serious resources. Will the old men be up for it?"

"At this point they'll do anything to save those oil revenues. Just don't skim so much that it's too obvious. Now then, what's your idea?"

Gotcha, thought Smith. "Let's call it, oh, I don't know...say, 'Operation Flamingo.' Here's what I'm thinking—"

Even as he laid out his plans, Smith made a mental note to stop back through Vegas in the second week in January. On the bright side, right after the incident, there'd be a dearth of johns roaming through the local cathouses. The price of pussy would drop to an all-time low.

CHAPTER 28

"Miss Guerrero, in your twenty years as a customs official here in the Port of Miami, you've built quite an impressive record for spotting illegals."

As Mr. Smith of the White House's Special Terrorism Task Force took her plump dimpled hand into his firm handshake, Rosa Guerrero felt she was going to burst with pride. Well, now the one her papa called *mi pequeña solterona*–"my little spinster¬"–was finally getting her due!

Mr. Smith had arranged to meet her right before she started her shift. They rendezvoused at a Starbucks in South Beach, right near Pier Park. There out beyond the shore, large ocean liners could be seen cruising languidly in or out of port. It was the perfect place to make his point: how she would be her adopted country's first line of defense for a new wave of terrorists, not from the Middle East—or even Cuba, the country she had left as a boat person—but from an even bigger threat:

Cuba's wealthier neighbor, Venezuela.

"You've seen how it has become a rogue nation," Mr. Smith declared. "How, for years, it's been propping up the dictator of your native land."

Just the thought of Padilla, that Castro wannabe, made Rosa's blood boil. She envisioned the boatloads that would soon be washing up along Miami's shores.

Boats carrying little girls and their parents—the best and the brightest, destitute and having to start their lives over again from scratch.

"This is a very special assignment, one that requires your total discretion." Mr. Smith lowered his voice and leaned in. The way he placed his hand on her shoulder encouraged her to do the same. "Our success depends on how well you do your job. At this point, no one—not even your direct supervisor, Mr. Cameron, will know your role in Operation Flamingo."

Rosa nodded. That was fine with her. Cameron was an idiot, just counting down the days until his retirement. If anything, *El Stupido* chastised her for the number of shifty characters she pulled over. Worse yet, if the aliens raised a fuss, he sided with them, not her. Once she caught him calling her a frustrated old maid behind her back. When she turned him in, all he learned in the mandatory two-week sensitivity training session was to ignore her, and to schedule her for even worse shifts. Yes, she was ready for the challenge of Operation Flamingo. Anything to get her out from under the thumb of that *cerdo machista*.

"We anticipate you'll find at least three or four a week, over the next four weeks," Mr. Smith continued. "Their M.O. is this: single males, mid-twenties to mid-thirties. All have blue or green eyes. All hail from small villages. You are to determine whether they have any family to speak of, either stateside or back home. If not, then they may be the men we are looking for. They will be working menial jobs, most likely on cruise ships. You should take the papers of anyone who fits this description, and keep them dockside. Then dial this special number and our interrogators will come to assist you. It's as simple as that."

Noting Rosa's wariness, Smith smiled and murmured, "Needless to say, with your extra duties will come additional compensation. Your salary is $42,000 a year, am I right? We will pay you a bonus of $2,000 for each bona fide terrorist you ID."

Four a week, at $2,000 a pop? That condo she longed to buy right there in South Beach would finally be within reach...

Suddenly Rosa frowned. As much as she wanted to help, a few too many inquisitions would have Cameron questioning her motives. She could just imagine his smirks, or some disgraceful utterance, just loud enough for her and her coworkers to hear, about how her time of the month was now in its third consecutive week. That filthy *pingita*.

"Of course I will do whatever my country needs. My boss, though, he can be—well, let's just say he's less patriotic. *¿Entiendes, Señor Smith?*"

"*Si, entiendo perfectamente.*" Smith's smile was reassuring. "All the more reason for Mr. Cameron's retirement to take place as soon as possible. It is all too obvious to my superiors that he is out of touch with the reality of our terrorist situation." He gave Rosa's hand a gentle pat. "And I can't imagine a better, more patriotic replacement than you."

Rosa couldn't contain herself. A spontaneous genuflection was followed by a bear hug that caught Smith totally off guard.

His first impulse was to reach for his gun. His second was to brush his hand across her nipple to determine if the rumors that Rosa Guerrero was still a virgin were true. Her gasp, followed by a shameful smile, told him it was.

Perfect. A fifty-year-old virgin. Playing her during the coming weeks would be a piece of cake.

After she delivered the goods, he'd thank her properly. Then he'd exterminate her afterward, of course.

No doubt about it, the last night of her life would end with a bang.

CHAPTER 29

Mr. Smith's raid on Titus Wainwright's two-hundred-acre compound off of State Highway 89 in the middle of the Arizona Strip took place during the wee hours in the morning of his honeymoon night with Tina, the newest and youngest of his sister wives.

The prophet, a renegade even within the Fundamentalist Latter Day Saints sect, had just mounted the thirteen-year-old girl for the second time when the door to the bedroom was blown off its hinges, and a SWAT team of eight men rushed in. Waving their high-powered rifles and shouting orders, they dragged Prophet Titus off the bed then pistol-whipped him in front of the shocked, whimpering girl. One of the men was thoughtful enough to toss the blood-smeared bed sheet to Tina before shuttling them both out of the room, through the family barracks, and out to join Titus's eight other wives and his twenty-six children on the bus that would carry them out of the compound.

Whereas the rest of the trespassers were dressed in heavy black body armor, helmets, and night vision goggles, the one waiting by the bus was dressed neatly in a dark suit and tie. The name on his wallet badge said SMITH.

Smith's satellite reconnaissance of the compound had intimated that it would make an ideal base in which to carry out Operation Flamingo. Now that he was on the ground there, he saw for himself that it was perfect. The large barracks were centered deep inside the two-hundred-acre spread so far off the two-lane road that it almost didn't exist. If it weren't for the barbed wire fence that went all the way around the property, no one would even know that the land wasn't part of the national park that bounded the desert on the southeast side.

"You got yourself quite a little kingdom of heaven out here in the middle of the bumfuck boonies, now don't you, Prophet?" Mr. Smith smirked at Tina in her bed sheet. Like most nonbelievers, this one was unable to comprehend Titus's hold over so many women, particularly the young ones. "Too bad you'll be stuck in a living hell for the rest of your life, and never be able to use it. Let's see now: We've got you on tax fraud. Hell, the income you've made from that call center boiler room you've been running out here in this godforsaken desert will put you away for a long time, say twenty or so years. There are also the multiple child rape charges to take into consideration. But if we put you away in Maximum, that's an automatic death sentence, you know, what with the way the general prison population feels about child molesters—"

Several of the older women started howling when they heard that. The old man keeled forward, clutching his chest. He prayed that the pain was a heart attack. Even that was better than the slammer...

"Tell you what, Mr. Wainwright. What if I made you an offer you'd be a fool to refuse?"

"What's that?" Titus croaked out.

"Just sign here. This acknowledges your crimes, and the forfeiture of your property to authorities. In exchange, we escort you and your, er, 'family' here over the border."

It was on the tip of Titus' tongue to tell the asshole to go fuck himself, but he thought better of it. His glasses had been crushed in the barracks raid so he couldn't read the paper placed in front of him. Still, he signed it anyway and handed it back to Smith.

The minute the pen left his shaking hand, he, too, was hustled onto the bus.

Nine hours later the bus should have arrived in the border town of Yuma, but it didn't. Smith made sure of that.

The bus would be found years later at the bottom of Lake Havasu, having fallen off the roadway above Parker Dam. It was presumed that the driver, one Titus Wainwright, had ignored the posted signs warning vehicles larger than passenger vans to keep off the narrow eight-foot-wide road.

None of its thirty passengers survived the fall into the world's deepest dam.

CHAPTER 30

His captors called him *Catorce*. It was the not-so-subtle way in which they kept track of their prisoners.

Those they hadn't already disposed of, anyway.

He would always remember the last time he was called by his real name, Carlos Suarez Rodriguez: It was by the plump middle-aged female Customs official, as she scrutinized his passport, then, hustled him into an interrogation room, where he was held for some seventeen hours until, scared and confused, he readily signed the papers presented to him—

Not realizing that he has just signed his death warrant.

For the next seven weeks, Carlos' home was a cell in the middle of the desert. Despite his isolation, Carlos soon realized that he was not alone. This catacomb of cells held some thirty or so other young Venezuelans with similar backgrounds, all of whom were being submitted to the same ordeal as he: savage beatings with electrical cords; sadistic threats from the merciless guards; and anti-Padilla rhetoric blasted over the intercom, twenty-four hours a day. Their diet consisted of an inedible gruel.

In no time at all they were all broken men.

Salvation came in the form of a priest, a Father Smith. In a calm voice, he implored their captors to stop all injustices, and for some reason, they listened to him. Fluent in Spanish, he prayed with the Venezuelans, got them to open up about their families and friends, their dreams and fears; inspired them to work with their captors in order to prove that they deserved to stay in the United States; moreover, that they should be fast-tracked to citizenship. Most of the men, Carlos included, were more compliant after that. Didn't their captors realize that they already hated Padilla? The fact that they had left everything behind to be here was proof enough of that. Perhaps what they were going to be asked to do in order to gain their citizenship wasn't so bad after all...

Yes, the *Venezuelaños* trusted Padre Smith. In fact, one of the men felt so comfortable with the Father that he divulged the escape plan of two others.

When the two men disappeared from camp, Carlos realized Smith wasn't really a priest at all.

By then it was too late. They were no longer men, but ghosts. They did anything and everything their captors asked of them. At their behest, Carlos even drowned one of the other *Venezuelaños* in a latrine trough.

He was rewarded with three blankets to keep him warm, and a chocolate bar.

And when five of the *Venezuelaños* were chosen to go with Smith, he knew that, soon, his own date with death was imminent.

CHAPTER 31

Ben's meeting with the Detroit union leaders did not go as well as he had anticipated, but it hadn't been a total bust. Eight years of a Republican administration whose policies had done little to help its workers retain their jobs made them wary of what he had to say about Andy Mansfield's *100 Percent Zero Emission Race* strategy to give a further boost to the American automakers' market share, let alone trust that Andy could get the car companies to agree to it.

The one glimmer of hope was that they'd rather have Andy as the Republican nominee than Talbot. So yeah, they were certainly open to some face time with Senator Mansfield, even a photo op in, say, late January, perhaps right before the Michigan primary.

Or as one of the union bosses put it: "You keep doin' what you're doin', you'll keep gettin' what you're gettin'. It's time for Detroit to shit or get off the pot."

A succinct, albeit colorful, metaphor.

The good news was that Ben was able to catch an earlier flight home. And since neither the senator nor his campaign staff was expecting him in the office until the next day, at ten at night it was still early enough to see if Maddy wanted some company.

Yeah, all right: a booty call.

It didn't occur to him to phone first. He'd come to know her work habits, her daily rhythm. Right now, he thought, she'd still

145

be in the middle of soldering her latest project. She would not have eaten all day, and would certainly appreciate him scrambling a few eggs into an omelet for her.

Perhaps even show her appreciation in some ingenious way.

Ben offered his taxi driver a tip as big as the fare if he got him to her place in ten or less.

Eight minutes later they pulled up across the street from her front door.

If he'd shown up even one minute later he would have missed seeing her out there, clenched in a passionate embrace with some tall drink of water. The two of them were sucking face so hard that in their rush to get inside and tear each other's clothes off, to go at each other like two pigs in heat, she fumbled as she crammed the key into the front door lock and it dropped onto the stoop.

It was too dark for any hope of seeing the bastard's face as he bent down to retrieve it for her. But it was not too hard to imagine the look on hers as she oh so lovingly stroked the back of his head.

That one move pierced Ben's heart like none other.

"Yo, bud, the meter's still running." The taxi driver was oblivious to her betrayal, to Ben's broken heart, until, through the rearview mirror, his eyes met Ben's.

"I'm... not getting out. One more stop, please. Georgetown."

The driver nodded.

By the time Ben looked back over at the couple, they'd already made it inside.

"Ride's on me," the driver said as he pulled up to Ben's place.

CHAPTER 32

It was easy for Ben to avoid her calls when he was on the road. Now that the campaign was heating up, now that Clyde Dooley had fallen to the sidelines and it was just a two-man race going into the primary, he had lots of organizing to do, lots of strategies to implement.

Lots of excuses not to call back.

At first the messages she left were casual. No pressure, no urgency, no inkling as to his state of mind, or lack thereof. By the second week of his boycott, she still kept it playful, but her questions were pointed, her tone concerned. "Hey, lover boy, what's with the silent treatment? Was it something I said?...Please call. I miss you."

By the week of Thanksgiving, she'd taken the hint.

He saved all her voice messages. That way, when he needed to hear her voice, he'd play them back, one after another, to remind himself of her betrayal.

On Thanksgiving, Tess and Bess made turkey and fixings for all the lonely souls on the campaign team, which was practically everyone. What comes first, Ben wondered, the lack of a home life, or the obsession to win some cause? He guessed the former.

Jesus, no matter how many wins we rack up, we're still losers.

Andy and Abby stopped by with a homemade pumpkin pie.

Seeing his boss's wife made him ache for Maddy.

"You're looking too thin these days," Abby murmured as she cut him a hefty wedge.

He nodded, but didn't say a word. He was afraid that, had he opened his mouth, he would have blurted out: *You were right about her. I wish I'd listened to you. Why couldn't she be more like you?*

The rest of the afternoon he avoided Abby's concerned looks as long as he could by feigning interest in the campaign gossip being bandied about the room. He tried his best not to make it obvious that he was avoiding her.

Until Abby followed him outside.

They stood there in silence for a long while, watching the pale pink afternoon light fade to deep lavender, until finally she came right out with it. "You hate me, don't you?"

His eyes opened wide with shock. "Why do you say that?"

"You know why. Maddy." She was staring off at the North Star, now puckering an indigo sky.

He didn't know what to say about that, so he decided to tell her the truth. "I did hate you, once. But now I know you were right. If it makes you feel better, I can tell you honestly that I don't feel anything at all."

She looked at him with those woeful blue eyes. Then without a word, she placed her hand in his.

He remembered the last time she touched him, how it filled him with longing. He held onto her hand as long as he could, or at least until he felt her shiver in the cool breeze.

Then he escorted her back inside.

While the other guests ate pie and made small talk, he slipped out the door.

She was there, waiting for him, when he got home.

"I made pie. Pecan. Eat it at your own risk." Maddy held it out to him with both hands—a peace offering with a burnt crust.

"I already ate. Abby made pumpkin." He enjoyed the fact that she winced when he said her sister's name.

She tossed the pie tin onto the table. Part of the crust fell off. Unfortunately, it was the part that wasn't burnt. "Oh? So they're in town. I thought they'd have flown down to North Carolina for the holiday, get in a few photo ops. A turkey shoot, maybe. You know, Andy's a crack shot. So is Abby, for that matter." It wasn't idle chatter, but a taunt.

"How about you?"

"Me? I make love, not war. Or don't you remember." She crossed her arms at her waist. "Ben, tell me what's wrong. What happened?"

"I saw him. With you. The Invisible Man."

The look on her face went from disbelief, to shame, to sadness. "Ah. So now you know. Does anyone else?"

"Seriously, Maddy, who else would give a shit?" He was tired of the games. He wanted to smack her then toss her out the door.

Or make love to her.

"But I thought—" Seeing his lack of comprehension gave her some semblance of relief. "Look, Ben, I don't know what you think you saw—"

"Maddy cut the bullshit." He tried to keep his voice as steady as possible. "It was the night I came home from Detroit. You were in your doorway. *With him.* You were kissing."

"I know when it was. That's how long it's been, between us." Her eyes begged for forgiveness. "Yes, we were kissing. But I was kissing him goodbye."

"Then why did you take him upstairs?" *Why did you stroke*

his head? Why do you love him, and not me?

"I wanted to...say goodbye." A small smile dusted her lips. "I would have done the same to you, if I'd known it was our last night together."

He grabbed her arm and yanked her to his side. "Quite a sendoff. Makes breaking up with you quite a treat, I can imagine."

Her palm hit him squarely across the face. She laughed cruelly as he reeled back in pain. "How's that? I guess it makes it even easier, in your case."

She almost made it to the door when he grabbed her. He had her down on her hands and knees in no time. As his hand snaked up her skirt, she arched her back at the sensation. Soon she quit struggling against his fierce strokes.

Knowing he would burst at any moment, he yanked up her skirt and straddled her. With each downward plunge, Maddy let loose with an ecstatic moan. Her vise-like grip on the head of his cock made him suck in his breath. Finally he couldn't hold in his own groans. Their savage duet built to a crescendo as he surged through her.

Spent, they tumbled together back onto the floor.

When finally he could speak, he said, "Did you really mean what you said, that it's over with him?"

"Yes—yes! It's over. He could never...love me." She wasn't facing him, but he knew, by the crack in her voice, that she was speaking the truth.

No one could ever love you like I do.

She must have known it, too. Which was why she nodded when he whispered into her ear: "Don't ever leave me."

Venezuelan Eco-Terrorists Killed in Arrest Raid

By THE ASSOCIATED PRESS

Filed at 11:14 p.m. ET, 12/23/--

Minneapolis (AP) — Five Venezuelan nationals, suspected of plotting a scheme to blow up Minnesota's Mall of America on the last Saturday of the holiday shopping season, were killed in a shoot-out with United States Homeland Security forces in the community of Richfield.

According to media reports, none of the suspects survived the shoot-out, which took place at their safe house. But apparently the mission of these self-proclaimed Venezuelan eco-terrorists was to protest "Imperialistic America's gluttony for the blood and oil of others."

Thirty-two plastic tubes found in a cabinet were filled with high-powered explosives, which were being mixed into shampoo bottles. An "off-the-record intelligence source" told CNN that Homeland Security suspects that Venezuelan president, Manolo Padilla, had funded the group.

Later that day—just in time for the evening news—the new Chief of Homeland Security, Arthur Chase, confirmed this, stating that a fax discussing wire transfers from individuals in Miami, and signed "Ponce"—a name believed to be one of terrorists' aliases—mentions a terrorist organization called the MPD, or Muerte a la Patria del Diablo, which translates into "Death to the Devil's Homeland."

As part of the investigation, the FBI concluded that at least $49,000 in wire transfers was sent from Venezuela to Mexico and Argentina to a "Pedro Duarte."

Vice President Talbot's presence at the press conference is evidence that the White House sees this as a serious threat to the country. "We must protect and defend our country, at all costs. I'm sure the Venezuelan people will welcome liberation from the tyrant dictator who now controls their government."

President Padilla denied any knowledge of the plot "concocted by the imperialist United States in order to invade Venezuela for its oil."

——————————

CHAPTER 33

After reading about the five Venezuelan nationals, Ben suddenly felt as paranoid as Fred.

"It's all such bullshit," chortled Fred, who, as usual, appeared at the Mansfield for President campaign headquarters after everyone but Andy and Ben had gone home. He was already digging into the bucket of chicken he'd brought with him. Ben would not have doubted in the least that the spy had a camera hidden somewhere inside their offices. While that should have bugged him, it only made him feel safer.

"What, are you saying that someone else was behind it?"

Fred and Andy exchanged glances. Andy shrugged. "It's an election year, isn't it?"

The two of them disappeared into Andy's office and shut the door.

Ben shook his head. Dirty tricks were a given. Considering all that had happened these past twelve months, he now laughed at his naiveté over his shock when their offices were bugged. But he still found it hard to wrap his brain around the concept that the sitting United States vice president had anything to do with black sites, or assassinations.

"Is Andy inside?"

Ben looked up to find Paul in the doorway. Since their lunch at the University Club, he'd made it a point to meet with Andy away from the Mansfield campaign headquarters. There were no more boys' nights out down at Bedrock Billiards.

That was fine with Ben. He nodded toward Andy's office. "Fred's with him. They don't want to be disturbed."

Paul frowned. "You shouldn't let Fred pull him away to play James Bond. That takes him off his game."

Ben agreed, but the last thing he'd do is let Paul know that. Paul squirmed whenever he felt he'd been left out of the loop. Between Ben and Fred, he was out a lot. "With what he's telling our boy, my guess is that Andy will win 'the game' hands down."

"What conspiracy theories are they ruminating about now?" Paul walked to the window and looked out into the pitch black.

For all Ben knew, Fred was blowing hot air. But that didn't matter. Ben was having too much fun watching Paul twitch. He shrugged. "Beats me. Something about the Minnesota terrorist plot. And if Fred's intel is right, guess who's the hero of the day?"

Paul didn't say anything but Ben knew he'd gotten his goat by the way the lawyer clenched his fist. "Well, then, I'm sure he'll be tied up for quite some time. I've got to get home to the wife. Just tell him I stopped by to give him some great news. The Allenbergs have agreed to throw a fundraiser in the second week of January. All big fish." He wrapped his cashmere scarf around his neck and tucked it under his camelhair coat. "I assume we'll see you there, too. Feel free to bring a date. If you can find one on such short notice."

Ben resisted the urge to bash the bastard's head up against the wall.

He grabbed his laptop and buried it into his satchel, but waited until Paul left the building before heading out the door. It had been a long day, and he was bone tired.

Except for whatever Maddy had in mind. Hopefully, something naughty.

The past four weeks had been perfect. No secrets, no worries. Okay, maybe a bit of drama. She seemed short-tempered lately, moody over the silliest things.

Like a real girlfriend.

For the first time in his life, he felt whole.

CHAPTER 34

"Mansfield knows about 'Flamingo.'" Talbot abhorred making eye contact with anyone, but this time, so that Smith would have no misunderstanding about his anxiety over the issue, he made sure to meet the other man's eyes in the rear view mirror when he broke that bit of news.

Nothing. Smith's eyes did not go wide, nor did they narrow. He didn't even blink, let alone give the limo's steering wheel an involuntary smack in frustration. If there was any reaction at all, perhaps it was the ghost of a smile that, for just one brief second, shadowed his lips.

Then again, maybe Talbot imagined that.

Usually he was impressed with Smith's nonchalance under stress. This time, though, there was too much at stake, and he wanted Smith to commiserate with him; to feel his pain, so to speak. Hell, for once—just once!— he wished the man would act like a human being, not the cold, calculating sociopathic killer he was. "So, what are we going to do about it?"

Smith kept his eyes on Talbot, ostensibly as reassurance that he was all ears, but actually so that the vice president wouldn't notice his finger slipping behind the rear view mirror. Talbot had heaved himself into the car and blurted it out so fast that for once, Smith hadn't had time to activate the digital recorder first. "That depends. How do you know for sure that Mansfield knows anything?"

"That twerp, Paul Twist. He's angling for U.S. Attorney General, once I get elected. Thinks I owe it to him, considering his Judas routine." Talbot shook his head in disgust.

"His stuff has been pretty reliable thus far. Go ahead and string him along until I can track down his source." Frankly Smith hoped Talbot would grant the kid his wish. It gave him a hard-on just thinking he could have one over on the head honcho in the Justice Department, particularly one who obviously had his own mole buried somewhere within the bowels of the Pentagon. "It means there's a leak in your organization."

"What makes you think the leak is on my side? It could be one of your cutthroats."

"My 'cutthroats' are pros who know how to keep their mouths shut. It's power players like you who feel the need to let someone know what you're up to, if only to stroke your own egos—or to save your own asses." Smith let that sink in. "In any event, I guess we have a little problem."

"What's this 'we' shit? It's your problem, not mine." Talbot poked Smith's headrest to make his point. "And it's fucking humongous. So fix it. And fast. I don't doubt for a second that Mansfield plans to use it against me. Against all of us. Besides losing the nomination, I can be tried for treason! Just remember—if the old men and I go down, so do you."

"Are you ordering me to exterminate Mansfield?"

"What, do I have to spell it out for you?" Talbot's shout certainly left no doubt of his intentions, either live or digitized. "You know, accidents happen to everyone. Even presidential candidates. Only don't make it a public assassination. The goal is to get rid of the problem, not make the man a martyr."

CHAPTER 35

Ben supposed it wasn't too odd that both Maddy and Andy had come up with the same idea for Abby's Christmas gift: an antique copperplate engraving of St. Paul's Basilica, from a little art gallery on Wisconsin Avenue in Georgetown. Apparently they were both with her when she had admired it, and each had taken special note of this.

To Ben's dismay, however, the one day he had off from the campaign to go Christmas shopping with Maddy was also the day in which Andy chose to shop for Abby, too.

Ben's hand, entwined with Maddy's, left no doubt of their relationship. It didn't help either that her head was snuggled against his chest.

The congenial smile on Andy's face dissolved instantly at the realization that they were together. What took its place was shock, then cool annoyance. Involuntarily he turned to go, but then he changed his mind and steeled himself forward toward them.

"Ben. Maddy." He nodded stiffly. "What a surprise."

Maddy's eyes could cut glass. "Good to see you, Andy. I was just buying a little something for Abby. Like minds think alike, I guess."

He reeled back at Maddy's smirk, as if he'd been slapped on the cheek. Then to save face, he glanced around the store, moving toward another of the etchings in the same set. Nodding after it, he shrugged. "This way she'll have a matching pair. Twins."

It was Maddy's turn to wince.

Ben looked from one to the other. It was on the tip of his tongue to ask what the hell was going on, and why it should matter that he and Maddy knew each other; more importantly, to ask what Maddy and Andy shared that they weren't telling him.

But before he could open his mouth to say a word, Andy nodded curtly and walked the second etching toward the saleswoman.

Ben shrugged. "I guess our cover is blown."

Maddy smiled. "Yeah, gee what a shame."

She didn't really sound upset, and for some reason that bothered him. "Do you think he'll tell Abby?"

"Who, him?" That set her off into gales of laughter. "Nah, he's not that stupid."

Ben wished he knew what she meant by that, but he knew better than to ask.

"So, this thing with Maddy: is it serious?"

Andy waited until the following night to broach the topic. He and Ben were working late in the campaign offices, going over the following month's travel itinerary.

Ben was relieved that now he didn't have to hem and haw or come up with some kind of bullshit to cover what had to be obvious to anyone who saw the two of them together: "We love each other. That's all that matters, right? At least to her, and to me."

There, he'd said it to someone other than Maddy.

He watched Andy's face as that sunk in, and wondered if it occurred to Andy that the two of them might one day be brothers-in-law—

"I'd like to ask you a favor. I'd—I'd like to ask you to leave her alone."

Ben couldn't believe what he was hearing. *What...the fuck? Leave her alone?*

He crunched his fist into a knot. He could imagine one that size in his stomach. "I don't understand."

"What I'm trying to tell you is that you're making a big mistake. Ben, please trust me on this."

"Senator, with all due respect, I don't think that's up to you to say. It's between Maddy and me."

"There's a lot about her you don't know. And should it ever—if Abby ever found out —"

Ben had never seen Andy pace the floor like that. *What's he not saying here?*

"Listen, Senator, Maddy and I are both grown-ups. We know what we're getting into here." Ben shook his head in disbelief. "Frankly I would think that you of all people would be happy for us."

"*Me?* Yeah. Sure. Ecstatic." Andy frowned and closed his eyes.

Fuck you, thought Ben. But what he said instead, though not so convincingly: "Thanks for the vote of support."

"Does Abby know yet?" The dread in Andy's voice was obvious.

The memories of his lie to Abby, about dropping his relationship with Maddy, ran over Ben like a bad chill. "She may have an inkling. But hey, feel free to confirm it, if you want." Considering Andy's reaction to the news, he could only imagine what Abby would say about it.

About his betrayal to her.

Andy's mirthless laugh made him wince. "No thanks. I'll leave that honor to you."

He dismissed Ben without a glance.

THE DAY AFTER CHRISTMAS...

CHAPTER 36

"Will you—will you marry me?"

Oh fuck it. No matter how many times he practiced it in the mirror that morning, he choked up before he got it all out.

Get over it, you lovesick bastard. You know she's going to say yes...

Bullshit. He didn't know what Maddy was capable of doing or saying at any given moment. And the moment he was most concerned about was now less than a week away:

New Year's Eve.

We met last year on that night. Since then, we've been through hell and high water. But it was worth it. She's worth it. What else can she say but 'yes'?

Ben had never been higher. Despite the hardball politics going on between Andy and Talbot, despite the dirty tricks and maligning gossip, the latest polls no longer showed Andy neck-to-neck with the vice president but firmly in the lead.

Even some of Talbot's stalwart donors were seeing the light and were now lining up behind Mansfield—just in time for the start of the primary season.

Best yet, the last month with Maddy had also been wonderful. So for sure her answer would be yes. Despite her recent peevishness, which seemed to come right out of the blue, even during their most mundane conversations.

And despite the way she teared up now at the drop of a hat, particularly after lovemaking.

Ben was no dummy. He knew those were the little hints women used when they thought it was time that the guy popped the question. Of course she was upset he hadn't done it before now. So yeah, it was time to take things up a notch...

Silently he checked off the items he'd planned for the big night. Dinner at CityZen; perhaps the tasting menu, accompanied by champagne. Then right before midnight, they'd finish up with a cocktail at the Sky Terrace in the Hotel Washington, just in time to see the midnight fireworks—

And that's when he would pull out the ring: a platinum band embraced in a cluster of diamonds. He remembered how it caught her eye as they had strolled by the window of Tiffany's in Chevy Chase.

After the fireworks, he was taking her to the Hay-Adams, where he had secured the presidential suite for their own personal fireworks—

Perfect.

What woman *wouldn't* say yes?

But first things first. Later that evening he'd call her, to see when she wanted to meet him at his place.

CHAPTER 37

Smith's man, Charlie, had no problem stealing a uniform from one of the two approved maintenance subcontractors allowed to service planes at that particular airport. The electronic gate key got him in with no hassles. But just in case anyone was around to ask questions, he dummied up a fake Airworthiness Directive and stuck it in his back pocket so he'd have it to wave under the alert bastard's nose, if need be.

The plane was located in one of the newer, larger hangars at the end of the third row, the one closest to the runway. The swipe card that opened the hangar's manual double door had already been coded to open on command. Once he was inside, he closed the door behind him.

The job was a piece of cake. First Charlie loosened a bleed clamp in the pressurization system, but just enough to ensure that, forty minutes into the flight—by the time the plane reached an altitude of 26,000 feet or so—the outflow valve would pop off. When that happened, the cabin would decompress immediately, and all hell would break loose.

Next he replaced the emergency oxygen tank with an identical one that was filled with nitrogen instead.

The pilot's emergency procedure was predictable. First he'd put on his oxygen mask, and instruct any passengers to do the same. Then he'd radio the tower for an emergency descent, and switch the transponder to the MAYDAY signal: SQUAWK 7700. If he was really quick, he might even have time to put power all the way back to idle, and pull out spoilers—

Before the toxic gas flowing into his lungs asphyxiated him.

Of course, if the pilot's body were to stay intact—fat chance of that, considering that the plane's angle would be steep upon impact—the amount of the gas found in his lungs would be too negligible to raise suspicions among the NTSB investigators.

In other words, the cause of the crash would stay a mystery.

Personally, Charlie hoped there wouldn't be too many passengers onboard. As a former flyboy himself, nothing annoyed him more than the media's endless ruminations about the amount of fatalities caused by "pilot error."

Then again, this time around he'd hate for them to suspect the truth.

CHAPTER 38

Ben worked until seven that evening. Even the campaign workers who hadn't already taken off to their home states had already left the office. Holiday lethargy kept the campaign momentum from moving into full swing. But Ben's family was Maddy, and he knew her work habits: she'd still be welding on her latest statue long into the night.

By the way she answered the phone, distant and annoyed, he knew something was wrong.

Immediately he began stuttering like a schoolboy, but he did get out the words "New Years Eve" and "dinner reservations" before she interrupted him. "Look Ben, I've been meaning to say something for a while now–"

Oh, crap.

Her tone of voice was the dead giveaway. He thought his heart would burst because it was beating so fast, waiting for whatever it was she was about to throw his way—

"I'll just come out and say it." She paused for what seemed like an eternity before saying the one thing he dreaded hearing: "I'm sorry Ben. But it's over."

"What? Are you crazy?"

"No. Just...bored."

Bored. With him. The thought stunned him into silence.

It was her turn to fill the void. She did it with a sigh. "You know what they say: It was fun while it lasted. But now it's time for...for a clean break. It's my very own New Year's resolution. Sorry, bad joke. Look, seriously, I've got to go–"

Just like that. *Finito...*

No way.

He had to hear it from her in person. If she saw him–broken, in pain–well then fuck it, okay if he got down on his knees...

Yes, he was even willing to *grovel* like some pathetic little schoolboy¬. Then maybe she'd change her mind.

He grabbed his coat and computer satchel and ran out the door, but he didn't get far. He slammed into a solid wall of humanity: Fred.

Remotely it registered in Ben's mind that something was terribly wrong, out of context: this sluggish bear of a man who epitomized nonchalance, was now swift and anxious.

"Is Andy here? *Quick–*"

Taking Ben's stunned silent shrug as a no, Fred pushed a large unlabeled manila envelope into his hand.

"Well, see that he gets this, okay? Tell him it's what he's been looking for. Tell him that–*that the Flamingo has landed.*'"

Then he disappeared, as if into thin air.

Fucking spook! I don't have time for his games. I've got to get to Maddy's...

Ben was still fumbling with his belongings when the elevator opened. As always, Fred was long gone. Like a good spy, he had taken the stairwell instead.

CHAPTER 39

Ben got to Maddy's place just in time to catch her walking out the door. She had her coat on, and her hands were full with her hat, gloves, a bulky purse, a large ring of keys, folders and envelopes—

—And a bright red suitcase.

Seeing it stopped him cold in his tracks. "Where the hell are you going?"

"Away." She stood there, waiting to see if he'd move out of her way. When he didn't, she sighed and moved forward.

He barred the door with his arm. It was on the tip of his tongue to ask with whom, but the words stuck in his throat.

He didn't have to ask. She read the jealousy in his eyes. "*Alone*, Ben. I'm going alone. I swear."

He didn't believe her. And from the smirk on her face, the one that proved she thought he was a loser, he then knew she couldn't have cared less.

So she's seeing someone else. She's probably been seeing him all along.

The Invisible Man.

He had been played. Used. He wanted to hit her. *Hard*—

Instead he pulled her down onto the floor as if she were an animal, hoping to make her feel just as hated and as humiliated, just like him.

Or to want him again. Because only he knew what she loved. So yes, he was going to give it to her, right there and then.

He knew she loved the way his mouth tore into hers, and the way his fingers snaked up her thigh until they found what they longed to stroke in her: hot and moist, there under her skirt—

She slapped him, backhanded across the mouth. The pain wracked his head. They both lay there, panting.

"Fuck it, Ben! Don't you get it? We're over! And you know what? *I'm relieved!* I could never love you—not in the same way. Don't you see that? Quit being so—so...pathetic."

Her words burned through his brain, dropping like hot coals down into his heart. It stopped him cold.

Slowly she moved out from under him. The pity in her eyes was what kept him from stopping her, from killing her right then and there.

Pathetic.

Because of you. You fucking bitch.

Maddy pulled herself together again, grasping for the things that had scattered around them in their tussle. "Look, I've got a long drive ahead of me—"

Fogged by his anger, slowly he picked up the things he had dropped—his keys, his coat, the envelope—and staggered out the door after her.

But when he got into his car, he couldn't—wouldn't—drive away. Instead he waited. Was she truly going alone? Or would someone pull up any moment and drive her away?

No, she was alone in her car when it careened from the curb. He waited until a bus passed, then pulled out, too, keeping her within sight. He couldn't shake the urge to go after her, to beg her forgiveness, to assure her that he knew she hadn't meant what she said—

But deep down inside Ben knew it was useless to pretend otherwise.

He watched as she turned onto the Roosevelt Memorial Bridge, but he didn't follow her. Instead, he drove past the exit, and circled home.

CHAPTER 40

Work. There was always work to do, to keep his mind off of Maddy.

Granted, because the whole world seemed to be on holiday, things had slowed to a crawl. Still, the first week of January was only a few days away, and with it came the Iowa caucus.

He flipped open his computer. Staring him in the face were files on the latest poll stats, the new speechwriter's handiwork, the volunteer rolls, next month's budget...

Good. Anything to keep my mind off that bitch...

It wasn't until eleven o'clock that night that he realized he had never delivered Fred's envelope to Andy.

Damn it! The Maddy debacle had knocked him for a loop. Frantically he looked around for the envelope. Where was it? Oh yeah, there, where he'd dumped his coat and his keys...

As always, Andy would be flying his own Cessna Mustang, taking it out of Manassas Airport. Ben could still catch him if he hurried.

The traffic was light enough that he made the forty-mile trip in the same amount of minutes, record time for that section of Interstate 66. There was only one very sleepy guard at the airport's security gate. Recognizing Ben, he waved him in.

Ben drove right up onto the tarmac. Andy was already in the cockpit, waiting for clearance onto the active runway. Abby was there too, in casual wool slacks, a white wool car coat, and her hair pulled back under a white French beret. A white suitcase was behind her seat.

Her hand was in Andy's, who was kissing it gently when he noticed Ben watching them. Just then Abby looked up, too—

Both froze. Their smiles slowly dissolved into blank stares. Abby, obviously upset, adjusted her glasses higher on the bridge of her nose as she turned away from Ben.

He was shocked at her chilliness.

I guess they're embarrassed because I caught them in such a tender moment...

Or maybe Andy told her about Maddy and me. Fuck it. If he wants to fire me, so be it.

But Andy said nothing. He didn't smile at him, either. Good. Business as usual.

What was it that Fred asked him to say? Oh yeah: "Flamingo," Ben muttered as he handed the senator the envelope.

Andy's stare hardened and he gave Ben a curt nod. He turned his back on both Abby and Ben as he stuck the envelope in his aluminum attaché case and stowed it under the seat. All the while, Abby pointedly looked away from Ben.

Yeah, well, a Merry Christmas and a Happy New Year to you, too.

On the drive back to Washington, Ben detoured into the Metro Center. He had heard some of the younger staffers talking about the POV Rooftop Terrace and Lounge, at the W Hotel. There were plenty of fish in the sea, and plenty of women looking to get laid—hell, especially on a cold, lonely week off.

Well, right now he needed some fun. And he needed to get drunk. So fuck Maddy. No, fuck anyone *but* Maddy. Particularly if the liaison rolled into a six-day holiday fuckfest.

Four scotches later, he only wanted Maddy, so he went home

alone.

CHAPTER 41

It was two in the morning when the fireman's bell went off by his head. Really it was his cell phone, but with the hangover he had, who could tell the difference?

When he picked it up, he realized it was the cell given to him by Andy, so that the two of them could stay in touch all the time.

"Your television, Ben. Can you hear me? Turn it on. And hurry, damn it!" It wasn't Andy's voice on the other end of the line, but Fred's.

Ben rummaged around for the remote, but he refused to turn on the light in order to find it because that would have meant going blind, if the scotch hadn't already accomplished that goal.

What came on was a newscast. The on-the-scene reporter was standing next to a field, flooded with lights from a fleet of emergency vehicles. "—crashed at about midnight in this deserted meadow, outside of Providence Ridge, Virginia. The presidential hopeful, a former Marine pilot, was flying his own plane, a Cessna. Though there is no official word yet, witnesses say that both Senator Mansfield and his wife were seen boarding the plane around midnight. Sadly, there is no word of survivors—"

What he was seeing on the screen, coupled with the sudden pounding in Ben's head, forced what was left of the scotch back up his throat. He knew he'd never make it to the toilet. Instead he puked in the wastebasket beside his bed.

179

"Did you give him the envelope?"

Fred's voice sounded far away.

Ben lunged for the phone. "Yes, just like you told me! Right...right before the plane took off—"

"Aw, *shit*! Fuck it...Okay, okay, listen up. Andy's plane was sabotaged! I got that from my inside source. That's not good for either of us, dude. And for some reason there's a witch-hunt going on over here at Langley, so I may have to lay low for a while. I'll be back in touch when things calm down. If you get a knock on the door, you know nothing. Do you hear me? Not a thing. *I never gave you that envelope.*"

"Okay, okay! I get it. But—but what if I need to get in touch with you?"

"Have someone you trust make the call to me at Langley. *But not you.* From a pay phone. Whoever it is should say that my nephew Teddy's soccer game on Saturday has been postponed so no need to pick him up at the field."

"Your nephew...a soccer game...got it. Do you really have a nephew?"

"Yeah. But he doesn't play soccer. Basketball's his thing."

Fred's voice was replaced by a dial tone.

Ben had just zipped up his jeans when the phone rang again. He was glad Fred had rung back because he was panicking, and still had a lot of questions. "Yeah, okay I get it—"

"Ben, Andy said I should call you if—"

Maddy. Her wracked sobs broke his heart. "Oh my god! Maddy! I'm so sorry, baby. About Abby. I'll be right there—"

"No—*NO!*" What, she still didn't want to see him? Then why was she calling? Why did she feel the need to hurt him all over again—

"Damn it Ben, *listen!* I—I'm not Maddy!...*I'm Abby!*"

Abigail?

"But ...Abby was on the plane! Abby is dead!"

"*What?...NO!* I wasn't on that plane with him!"

Ben shook his head. "I saw her on the plane myself, right before takeoff! In the cockpit with Andy—"

"*Ben, listen to me!* THAT WAS NOT *ME*."

"Then who..."

Maddy.

Maddy was ...with Andy? But why...

Because Andy was the Invisible Man.

Andy—the Boy Scout, the loving husband. So Mr. True Blue was just as big a player, just as big a liar, as any other candidate—

And Maddy was his pliant willing whore, waiting at his beck and call.

And I was her whore.

It was a long time before he realized the howl piercing his heart was his own.

It all came back to him: How, on that very first night they met, at the bar outside the ballroom for Andy's New Year's Eve fundraiser, she tried to hide her bitterness with coy flirtation. Then, when their one-night stand became an obsession for them both, she insisted they tell no one about it, no matter how sincere he was about his love for her.

She didn't love me. She used me. To make him jealous.

In that regard, Andy had been telling the truth the night he tried to warn Ben about her.

Well, he was right.

He remembered the smirk Maddy gave him when he suggested that she go on the road with him. He had no doubt she mentioned that to Andy.

I'll just bet the two of them laughed their heads off. How they were pulling the wool over my eyes. Mine, and Abby's—

Abby's own heartbroken moan brought him out of his pain.

She's put two and two together, he thought. She knows it was Maddy. With her Andy.

That cocksucker. That fool. How could he have done that to her—with her own twin sister, no less?

Because he couldn't choose between them: Abby was the tonic: sweet, sincere, and loving; whereas Maddy was the addictive drug, the naughty obsession, the vulnerable child.

He had loved them both.

I can see why.

Ben remembered his own attraction to Abby. The guilt of his betrayal to her—they had *all* betrayed her—roused him out of his pain.

Well, she needs me now, more than ever.

"I'll come right over," he murmured into the phone.

"No. The press is all over here! I can sneak out the back. Trust me, I've done it before. I'd prefer to meet you...where? Maybe Maddy's?"

He croaked in agreement. Then he hung up. Yeah, it was good he was getting out of there. He couldn't stay in the room any longer. It reminded him too much of the last time he made love to Maddy.

Then it dawned up him where he was headed next.

He threw up again.

CHAPTER 42

Captured in the moonlight pouring into Maddy's studio, it was easy for Ben to mistake Abigail Vandergalen Mansfield for the love of his life.

It seemed like an eternity before she lifted her bowed head. He noticed she wasn't wearing her glasses. He imagined that the tears, streaming down her cheeks, had made that impossible. The scarf on her head covered her hair completely. While it gave her the anonymity she sought during this crisis, it so clearly exposed the facial features she shared with her sister—the high cheekbones, upturned nose, and those beautifully arched brows above her wide eyes.

He tried to stifle his heartbroken groan but he couldn't.

It roused her from her trance. Seeing this, he forced himself to say, "I'm...sorry."

"Why? Because she was on the plane with him, as opposed to me?"

He winced, not because of the sharpness of her tone or the piercing scrutiny of her question, but from the precision in which she exposed the truth.

Yes, he wished Maddy were here with him, now.

His reaction brought a tremble to her lips. It startled him to think she was actually hurt by this truth. Of course she is hurt, he reasoned. She just found out her husband betrayed her, with her own sister.

That Maddy had been loved by two men.

The same two men who had betrayed Abby.

Despite the pain it might bring her, he had to ask, "Why weren't you there, with him?"

The tears were falling again. She wiped them away with shaking palms. "It wasn't supposed to be more than a quick trip home, just overnight. He claimed he had an opportunity to meet with some key donors. We've both been on the road so much this past year. He was worried about my...my stamina. It was his suggestion that I stay home. I guess we now both know the real reason why."

"So you never had any suspicions about them?"

She raised her head in order to look him straight in the eye. "None. Never. I presume you hadn't either."

His cheerless laugh bounced off the high bare walls. "Trust me, had I known, I wouldn't have been running your husband's campaign." He was almost tempted to add, *And when Andy found out about it, he threatened to fire me if I mentioned it to you,* but thought better of it. She was devastated enough already.

It hurt him to see her crying like that. And yet, he had so many questions for her. "I just don't get it. She mentioned her 'Invisible Man' to me the first night you and I met, when Andrew hired me to run his campaign. So it had to be going on for some time. Surely you must have had some inkling about it. Women's intuition? Something? *Anything?*"

"I had trust. Fifteen years of it. I thought that counted for something." The iciness in her blue eyes sliced right through him. "Then again, I'm not as cynical as you. Which begs the question: considering the twelve months you've been at their beck and call, I'm surprised you didn't pick up on it, either—"

Her angry rant was interrupted by the buzzing of a cell

phone.

It was sitting on Maddy's coffee table.

Ben and Abby stared at each other.

"Is that yours?" they said in unison then they answered each other by shaking their heads.

"Answer it," Ben said. "But...do it as if you're Maddy."

Abby blanched but nodded. She cleared her throat before hitting the speaker button, and answering boldly, "Yeah, who is it?"

My God, if I didn't know better I'd think she was Maddy, he thought.

"Yes, this is—Maddy Vandergalen...Sorry I've missed your calls. I've just come in from—from out of town. Yes, I—I've just learned about the crash....Richmond Morgue? Of course, I'll be there. Let me write down that location."

While Abby grappled frantically through the clutter that filled the top of Maddy's desk, Ben plucked a pen and a notepad from the drawer and handed it to her.

"Alright, got it...Yes, thank you." Abby clicked off the phone, then turned to Ben. "That was the NTSB. Because of the fire, there's not much left of the...their remains. They've been moved from the crash site in Providence Forge, to the Richmond coroner's office." She melted into a chair. "I don't know if I can keep this up."

Ben knelt down in front of her. "If Fred is right and the plane was sabotaged, we don't want Andy and Maddy's...their relationship...to overshadow the investigation of the plane crash. As the next of kin, they'd give Maddy his belongings. Fred needs us to retrieve the envelope I gave Andy, right before takeoff."

"Fred is never wrong. If only—if only he'd gotten to Andy before...they were murdered." She buried her head in her hands and sobbed.

Ben wished he could do something for her, other than just stand there, watching helplessly.

Finally she lifted her face, her eyes were glassy, her smile thin and brittle. "My hair. Before we leave, I'll have to dye it and cut it."

"The convenience store around the corner is open twenty-four seven. I'll see if they have any hair color. I can guess the shade." That sounded stupid, but he'd heard you had to keep talking to people who were in shock, and it was all he could think of to say. He wished she'd stop shaking.

He wished he could hold her until she did.

But even if she appreciated it at first, she'd soon presume he was pretending she was Maddy.

She'd be right.

I'm a sick fuck, he thought.

As if reading his mind, she stood up. "You knew her so well, I'm sure you'll have no problem picking out her exact shade." Crossing her arms over her chest, she added, "Lock up after yourself. When you get back, leave it outside the bathroom. I'll come down when I'm ready to leave."

She didn't wait for his reply. Instead, she grabbed the scissors off the desk and without giving him a second glance, she started up the circular staircase.

CHAPTER 43

The hair color Ben brought back with him was a brown that was almost black, except for the auburn highlights that gave Abby's now razor straight hair a glossy sheen. She'd managed to cut and shape it into Maddy's signature cut—long bangs, with the rest of her hair angled sharply from her chin line to the nape of her neck.

When Abby walked out of the bedroom, she was wearing a pair of Maddy's tight black leather jeans. She had paired them with a lacy black tank top, worn under a black leather jacket. She sat down at the desk, where she applied a darker eye liner and a smokier eye shadow. Then with shaking hands, she put on Maddy's colored contact lenses so that they were no longer sky blue, but green like wet moss.

They were Maddy's eyes.

The final touch was the dark dot she placed to the left side of her mouth, to simulate Maddy's mole.

When she turned to face Ben, he could have sworn she was his Maddy.

Neither of them said a word during the first hour of the ride south to Richmond. Ben attributed Abby's silence to the fact that, like him, she'd had too little sleep.

That, and she was steeling herself for the performance of a lifetime.

Or maybe she found him too reprehensible to talk to.

This was fine by him. He was glad to keep his mind on driving and his eyes on the road, now that she had so completely transformed herself into the woman he had loved and lost.

By the time they approached the Richmond city limits, morning traffic had slowed to a crawl, but their pace was smooth enough that she lowered the passenger seat visor in order to use the mirror to apply lipstick.

He hadn't meant to, but he couldn't help but glance over at her. "That doesn't work," he muttered.

She glared over at him. "I beg your pardon?"

"The shade you're using. It's all wrong. Maddy would never wear something so... *pink*."

"Oh? Forgive me! Perhaps I should have let you pick out my make-up, too." She tossed the lipstick back into her purse. "I take back the offer. You'd enjoy it too much."

He braked the car so quickly that she grabbed the dashboard in order to right herself.

"Obviously my feelings for your sister disgust you. Maybe it would be better if I pulled over and let you out," Ben muttered.

Abby opened her mouth to say something, but then shut it. When finally she found her voice, it came out as a meek whisper. "I'm sorry, Ben. I know you're angry. Well, I am, too, Ben. I'm angry that I've lost my husband. I'm upset I've lost my sister. And yes, I've been blaming you when in truth I'm mad at Andy." She slipped down in her seat, deflated. "No, if I'm to be honest, I'm angry at Maddy. She was spellbinding. Or at least, men thought so. You may have been the last, but you certainly weren't the first."

Ben frowned. "Tell me about it. She had her charms, but you aren't without your own, Abby. Andy loved you. Despite his...his attraction to Maddy, he married you, not her. And he didn't ask for a divorce."

She slumped down in her seat. "Because it would have been political suicide. We both know that."

"Odds are he would have survived it. Dole did. So did Gingrich, not to mention Mark Sanford." He shrugged. "Andy called you his 'waypoint.' He claimed you were the one who kept him on the straight and narrow; that you were the one who kept him in check. Whatever hold Maddy had on him, it wasn't strong enough to take him from you."

"You expect me to find solace in that, don't you? Believe me, I wish I could, but I can't. Despite our estrangement, I'd always hoped Maddy knew I loved her; that when she was finally ready to talk through her anger, I'd be there to listen. Now I see she only wanted one thing from me—my husband." Abby pursed her lips. "Maddy could have had any man, but she set her sights on Andy. Why is that? Did I commit some slight that deserved such disregard?"

"Maybe Andy was the cause of the rift. Didn't Paul Twist introduce you to Andy? Was Maddy there, too?"

"No. The introduction happened after I'd graduated from Sarah Lawrence. By then Maddy was in New York, caught up in the art scene there. We had already grown apart, in our teens."

"What caused the rift?"

"I wish I knew." Her hands, clutched in despair, fell to her side. "After our parents died, we were raised by our aunt, Lavinia, on her estate, Asquith Hall. Back then it was considered the country: Northern Virginia before the Beltway suburbs built up around DC. As you can imagine, the tragedy drew us together. We were inseparable, that is, until the summer we turned fifteen."

"What happened then?"

"Uncle Preston suggested we spend the summer in New York. He'd be working out of the firm's New York office. He keeps an apartment on the Upper West Side. I was shy, and I loved the fact that being out in the country took us out of the spotlight. But

Maddy jumped at the chance to go. When Maddy came home, she was a different person. Aloof. Worldly." Abby shrugged. "Bitter. She said she'd met someone she liked, and she was head over heels for him. She never said, but I presumed it was one of the summer interns in Uncle Preston's New York office. I guess he broke her heart. I'm sure he expected more from her than she was willing to give him. You know...sex." She blushed. "In any regard, after that summer, things were never the same between us."

"Wasn't Andy an associate at your uncle's firm? Could they have met then?"

No, of course not!" Abby shook her head adamantly. "They met through me—at our wedding rehearsal, in fact. I mean, yes, he worked for Uncle Preston, but from what I remember, during that particular summer, he was still clerking for some federal judge."

She stared out the window, as if the memory could be found among the faces on Richmond's bustling streets. "Besides, if they had been dating before he met me, I would have known about it, right? I mean, why would they have kept it secret?" Abby wrinkled her brow in thought. "He would have never asked me out if he was in love with my sister. And if he had the audacity to do so, I would have never gone out with him. I loved Maddy too much to hurt her."

If only Maddy had felt the same way, she'd be here instead of you, Ben thought.

Now that they were in front of the coroner's office, he could bury this regret within the business at hand. "We're here, Abby. I hope you're ready for your close-up."

Andy's sister-in-law is quite a looker, thought Smith. Hey, maybe she'd be up for some consolation sex. She'll need it, after she sees what kind of condition Mansfield and his wife are in.

She was with some guy, but by their body language, he could tell they had nothing going on between them.

He recognized the man—Mansfield's campaign manager, Ben Brinker. Smith wished he could hear what Brinker was saying to the lead FAA investigator, but if he were any closer, he'd draw attention to himself, something he couldn't afford to do. With his tidy, nondescript suit and dark glasses, he'd given the Richmond coroner's staff the impression that he was with the NTSB security detail, which in turn thought he was with Homeland Security.

It was on days like today that his collection of official badges paid off in droves.

Thus far, site investigators had come away with the conclusion he'd hoped for: pilot error, which sent the plane into a nose dive. In fact, the crash had created such an inferno that everything inside it had been incinerated.

This was a relief to Smith, more so because the Ghost Squad had been hacked.

The discovery had been made only a few hours ago. The file on Operation Flamingo was among the breached files.

The good news was that the file had been embedded with a security worm. The bad news: the trail ended at Langley. From what his tech ops could tell, it had been opened by only one person: a CIA agent named Fred Hanover.

Smith's asshole puckered when intel on Hanover showed him to be Mansfield's closest friend. Immediately he put a couple of ghosts on Hanover's trail, but Better Off Dead Fred must have sniffed them out, because he flew the coop.

Did he have a chance to brief Mansfield on Flamingo? Smith wondered. Even if he had, that dirty little secret was now as dead as the senator himself.

Apparently the Mansfields' charred remains weren't much to behold. He didn't have clearance for either the evidence room or the morgue, but Smith had positioned himself so that he could see through the glass wall that separated the morgue from the hallway he was supposedly guarding. The FAA coroner unzipped one of the body bags. The Vandergalen woman gasped, but stood her ground. No such luck when the medic opened the second bag. She turned her head and ran out of the room.

He was having so much fun watching Mansfield's sister-in-law heave her breakfast in the corner of the evidence room that he almost missed seeing the investigator hand Brinker something—

An aluminum briefcase.

Shit, it must have belonged to Mansfield, thought Smith. A cold trickle of sweat went down his spine. What if evidence of Flamingo was inside?

Smith followed as Brinker took both the briefcase and grieving woman out of the building, but by the time he got to his car, they were already a few blocks down the street. Two tractor-trailers and an old woman in a PT Cruiser made sure he missed the light that would have put him on the expressway ramp, directly behind them.

That's okay. He knew where to find them.

"You wouldn't happen to know the code to open Andy's briefcase, would you?" Ben waited until they were almost in Fairfax before asking Abby.

She'd quit sobbing only half an hour ago. The whole time she hadn't said a word. She just stared straight ahead.

Now she turned to him. With a voice lacking any emotion, she said, "It's the date he earned his wings as a Marine Corps fighter pilot."

"Reach in the back. Open it."

To do so, she had to unbuckle her seat belt, hoist herself onto her knees and turn around in order to grab it from the floor, behind her seat.

Instinctively his eyes were drawn to the rear view mirror, but he jerked his head to the road again when the thought hit him, *Maddy's jeans do her justice.*

When she swung the case over, it sideswiped his head. "Sorry," she murmured, but he didn't believe her.

Maybe she read my mind, he thought.

A moment later she had it open. "What are we looking for?"

"Just before takeoff, I gave Andy a manila envelope. It came from Fred. Inside was information on something called Operation Flamingo. Fred's instructions were that it was for Andy's eyes only, so I didn't open it. But if it had anything to do with Andy and Maddy's deaths, I think we should know about it."

She filtered through the case. "There are four envelopes in here."

"It should still be sealed up. There is no label. I don't think he had time to open it before take-off."

""Three are unopened, and unlabeled." Abby opened one and shook her head. "It's the speech that was prepared for tonight's event," she muttered, as she reached for another. "This second one has some polling figures. So, I guess three's the charm." She cracked the seal on the final envelope and scanned the pages in her hand. "Pull over, Ben."

Her tone was ominous enough he jerked the car onto the shoulder of the road and let the car roll until it slowed to a complete stop. "What is it?"

She didn't answer. Instead she handed him the paper in her hands.

It wasn't at all what he expected. It looked official, and was marked "Confidential," but it wasn't a government document.

It was a medical form. A pregnancy test.

The patient, M. Elaine Vann, was eleven weeks pregnant.

Who the hell was Elaine...

Maddy.

Maddy...had been *pregnant*?

The thought that she'd been carrying his child washed over him like a cold wave of bittersweet regrets—

"It was his? Not mine?" The revelation slammed into his gut like a fist.

"She must have thought so." Abby stared out the window. "Otherwise why would Andy have her test results?"

"Oh...shit! Wait! She didn't give this to him. I did." Ben slammed his hands on the steering wheel. "Yesterday afternoon, she called me to tell me she was ending our relationship. I was so angry that I went over to her place. I thought I could—that I could force her to change her mind. When I got there, she was rushing out the door. She had a suitcase with her, and a bunch of other things in her hands. I presume she was rushing to meet her invisible man. But I wouldn't let her go until we—" he paused, embarrassed, "—well, until we made love, one last time. She— *we*—dropped everything. On the floor. I guess we exchanged envelopes without realizing it."

"Oh Ben, I'm so sorry." Blushing, Abby looked down at her lap. "Knowing Maddy, nothing would have changed her mind. Not when she was able to give Andy something I never could. A child."

She's trying to comfort me, but I should be comforting her, he thought. Then it hit him: Would Maddy have tried to get pregnant if he hadn't let it slip about Abby's fertility efforts?

He looked down at the test results. Yes, a DNA test had been performed, too. The results show fifteen genetic markers. Were they his, or Andy's?

Abby frowned. "If she took Fred's envelope by mistake, it may have burned up in the crash, along with the rest of her things."

"That's the strange part. She left much earlier than she needed, in order to make the flight. And on the plane, she wasn't dressed in the same outfit she left in. She was dressed to look like you. Not only that, the bag she had with her was different." He stared at the DNA analysis. "Maybe she didn't want to share the test results with him after all."

Abby shrugged. "That's possible. Even if she were to hide the knowledge of her child's DNA, she may have felt that the day would come when she'd need proof of her child's paternity."

"In other words," Ben interrupted, "Maddy might have hidden the envelope. But where?"

Abby shook her head. "I don't know."

Ben's cell phone buzzed. Caller ID showed it was Sukie, so he answered it on speaker.

"Ben, thank God I found you!" He was touched by the concern in her voice. "Where are you?"

"With...with Maddy. I took her down to Richmond, to identify the senator's body. What's up?"

"She's with you? Good, because Preston Alcott is worried about both of you. He wanted you to know that he petitioned the FAA to release Andy's and Abby's remains for burial. The funeral will take place tomorrow, two o'clock at Arlington National Cemetery. He feels the sooner they're laid to rest, the less chance for the media to make a circus out of the tragedy."

"Yeah, right," he muttered then hung up.

In other words, the sooner the public forgets about Andrew Mansfield, the sooner Talbot locks down the GOP nomination.

But he could tell Abby had different thoughts on the matter. "May they both rest in peace," she murmured.

He wondered when the thought would hit her that Maddy was being laid to rest in the gravesite meant for her.

CHAPTER 44

Unlike the night in which they died, the December day in which Andrew Mansfield and the woman he loved were to be laid to rest had a crisp blue sky and only a whisper of a breeze.

Abby hid her damp red eyes behind the largest pair of sunglasses she could find in Maddy's accessories drawer. Maddy owned a lot of black clothes, but none of them were exactly funeral attire. For the graveside service, she chose a black lace wrap blouse, which she wore with a short tight black skirt which hugged every curve of her body. Ben assumed Abby's blushing cheeks were the result of the much too visible cleavage Maddy's black push-up bra gave her. She paired black seamed stockings with four-inch black heels. Ben thought she'd made the right choice, considering the only other alternative: Maddy's thigh-high black patent leather boots with a five-inch platform heel.

"The whole thing will take three hours, tops," he said as way of comforting her.

She shuddered. "I don't know how she does...how she did it. Every piece of clothing she owned was designed to make men take notice of her."

One man in particular, Ben thought. And it wasn't me.

Abby stared into the mirror as she applied a fake beauty mark. "Many of our friends weren't too fond of her."

"Maybe that's for the best. It means you won't be the center of attention for very long. They'll pay their respects and then run in the opposite direction."

"I guess you're right." She sighed. "At least Aunt Lavinia won't run away from me. She loved us both, dearly. She'll want to comfort 'Maddy'."

"You should let her. Anything that gives you solace during this time should be welcomed."

"It's good to hear you say so." For the first time since this ordeal, Abby graced him with a slight smile. "I'll be relieved to share my secret with someone."

Ben shook his head. "Sorry Abby, but you can't tell Lavinia about this. If Fred is correct, the less people who know, the better, at least until we get his intel to the right people. The last thing you'd want is to put her life at risk."

Abby's face fell. "Yes, of course you're right. But certainly Uncle Preston should be told the truth. I'm sure he can help us—"

"Don't you get it? We'd be putting a target on his back! He may feel invincible. Most of his kind do. But if Talbot is behind some illegal act—if Talbot is behind Andy and Maddy's death—do you think he'll allow Preston to talk him into doing the right thing? If anything, Preston becomes just another liability. Just like Andy. Not to mention you and me. Why do you think Fred is on the run?"

Abby nodded. She got it. The price for truth was too high.

It had already cost her too much.

So near, and yet so far. That was how Abby felt about everything and everyone around her.

With Maddy's contacts in her eyes, her depth perception was just a bit off. Those standing farther away—Andy's senate staffers, his campaign staff, his senate colleagues—seemed fuzzy, out of focus.

Those who stood close by—Aunt Lavinia, Uncle Preston, Paul Twist, his wife Laura, and Ben—were dizzyingly clear, as if watching a film in 3D Hi-Def.

Abby's head throbbed.

Upon arrival, everyone had been given two pink-tipped yellow roses, a hybrid known as Chicago Peace. It was known to be Abby's favorite. She'd used it in her bridal bouquet. Through Maddy's lenses, the roses she held in her hand looked surreal.

Her aunt was devastated, and certainly too numbed to do anything other than cling to her brother. Ben is right, Abby thought. I can't burden Aunt Lavinia with my secret. She's too fragile to take the shock of it all.

Whereas Paul was nervous, her uncle's demeanor was stoic. As always, he was the calm center in any emotional storm roiling around the Vandergalens.

Poor Ben was simply bereft. His eyes were red-rimmed, but he held his head high. She didn't blame him for keeping his gaze far away from Maddy's coffin. Thinking of Maddy and Andy's decimated bodies would strip both Ben and her of the memories they cherished most: their loved ones' faces, their voices, their smiles—

Their touch.

She tuned out her minister's sermon. The last thing she needed to hear was her own eulogy. Having her good deeds recalled for those present only made her feel frustrated that she'd been so naïve about the world.

At least, as it pertained to Andy's world. The cutthroat gamesmanship of politics. The coldhearted calculations of men who would do anything to stay in power.

Even if it meant murder.

She'd always been proud of Andy's political legacy. She'd adored him as a husband, craved him as a lover. But learning about his infidelity had devastated her. She longed to see him as a victim of a jealous, conniving sister, but deep down in her heart, she knew that just wasn't the case. If anything, Maddy had done her best to live her own life, far away from her sister's. She'd kept away from DC's social scene, its I'll-scratch-your-back-if-you-scratch-mine cronyism. Her rare appearances at family functions came at Aunt Lavinia's behest. If she came to Andy's political events, it was only because Uncle Preston insisted that Maddy "support the public face of our family."

Maddy came, albeit unwillingly.

At least, that was Abby's presumption until now.

She wondered if Maddy's obvious boredom at such gatherings had been merely an act. Now she realized Maddy's indifference to Andy had nothing to do with her disgust of politics in general, let alone his party's in particular.

Worse yet, she now understood the reason for Maddy's pitying glances.

She was contemplating Andy's reaction to the news of Maddy's pregnancy when it occurred to her that the minister had stopped speaking. She looked up to find everyone's head bowed in silence.

Except for Ben's. His was looking at her with the same look of pity she'd seen in Maddy's eyes.

She dropped a rose on each casket then walked off. For propriety's sake, she resisted the urge to run away. That, and she was afraid she'd trip in those damn four-inch heels and tear her too tight, too short skirt.

I should have kept my head down, Ben thought. She thinks I hate her.

I don't. Frankly I admire her for the way she was holding it together—until now.

I can't have her falling apart at the seams. Not now, when everything is going to hell. I need her to bring her A game.

He didn't chase after her. It would have drawn too much attention to them both, which was the last thing he wanted to do.

He could certainly understand why Fred wasn't there. A part of him wished he could have stayed away, too. The part that didn't want to get killed.

Throughout the funeral he'd been scanning the crowd, picking out the faces that were known to him. A group of blue-haired old ladies was sniffling. He presumed they were there to support Lavinia. They were standing behind President Barksdale and the first lady.

Alcott had certainly pulled out all the stops.

Vice President Talbot had also come to pay his respects to his political opponent. He was surrounded by a Secret Service detail. It was the faces he didn't recognize that worried him. How many of the Ghost Squad were there among them?

One face did look familiar, but he couldn't place it. The man's black suit was topped with dark glasses and a chauffeur's cap. He was standing near Talbot's coterie, yet far enough from the others that he might not have come with them at all.

Suddenly he remembered where he'd seen the man: in the Richmond coroner's office.

Is he staring at me? Ben wondered. It was hard to tell, since his shades were too dark to show his eyes.

No, the man's head was angled and moving ever so slightly.

Ben tried to follow his gaze. He realized the man's eyes must be following Abby, who was making her way back to the limo assigned to them. The man's lips were moving.

He must have been whispering into a tiny hidden microphone.

Just then a large woman standing in the midst of Lavinia's friends lifted the veil from the brim of her hat and winked at Ben.

Is that old bat flirting with me, he wondered.

Apparently not. Just giving him a warning. *Don't stare.*

The woman was really Fred, in drag.

Ben got it: the warning was about Talbot's chauffeur, who was now staring directly at him.

Realizing Ben was staring beyond him, the chauffeur turned his head sharply, to see who Ben had been watching a moment before.

But Fred was no longer there. It was as if he'd disappeared into thin air.

Too bad he can't take me with him, Ben thought.

Instead, he'd have to hide in plain sight from the Ghost Squad. At least now, thanks to Fred, he knew who was after him.

He'd make sure Abby knew, too.

"We have a slight problem, sir," Smith said.

He had waited until he'd driven Talbot halfway to the mourners' reception at Alcott's Georgetown estate before coming out with it.

Talbot looked up from his cell phone, where he had been monitoring the fawning Twitter comments to his gravesite sound bite. "What the hell are you talking about? Mansfield is dead and buried, along with anything he may have discovered about Flamingo. It's only a matter of time before the leak in Langley is plugged." He guffawed at the cleverness of his double entendre. "Case closed, as far as I'm concerned."

"He had a briefcase with him on the plane. Fireproof. It's now in the hands of Brinker, the guy who ran his campaign. He accompanied the Vandergalen woman to view the bodies."

Talbot's smile faded. "What are you waiting for, a written invitation to get it?"

"Not at all. In fact, I've got a few boys tossing his place as we speak." Smith paused. "If it turns out he's got the goods, I presume he's set us back to square one."

"Not if he hasn't released it." Talbot turned back to his phone. "Just take care of him."

"You mean 'them,' don't you? If he opened it while she was around, she's a liability, too."

"If that turns out to be the case, just take care of business." Talbot shrugged. "Alcott's fond of the girl, but he'll get over it."

"But of course, now that I have the Talbot seal of approval," Smith murmured. "Consider it done."

CHAPTER 45

"I'm sorry for your losses, Maddy."

Abby turned around when she recognized Paul's voice. The history they shared, and his brotherhood with Andy gave her reason to believe the sincerity she heard in his voice. Thankful, she smiled up at him.

"Let's go outside for a moment, to talk," he murmured. He waited for her nod before taking her arm and steering her out of Alcott's crowded living room, toward the library down the hall.

She thought nothing of the fact that he sat down beside her on the leather Chesterfield couch that faced the large roaring fireplace. When he put his arm around her shoulder, all she thought about was how appreciative she was that Andy's close friend understood her sister's anguish, and was there to comfort her.

What wasn't so comfortable was how matter-of-factly he crammed his tongue into her mouth.

She was too shocked to do anything. At first. He got the message that he'd overstepped all boundaries of propriety when she bit down hard on his tongue.

He yelped and jumped up off the couch.

"What the hell are you doing?" She glared at him.

"What do you think? I'm comforting you in your hour of need!" He spit blood with his words. "You know, for old time's sake."

So Maddy had been Paul's lover, too, once upon a time.

The thought made Abby bow her head in disgust. "How dare you, Paul! And today, of all days."

He smirked despite his pain. "I guess you're right. Forgive me. I thought you would be missing him by now and would appreciate a little company. You know, for old time's sake."

The next thing she knew, he was on top of her again, cupping her breast with one hand, while the other roamed between her legs. She struggled, but he was much too strong for her. She closed her eyes as his fingers grappled with the buttons on her blouse—

And then he was gone.

She opened her eyes in time to see Ben punch Paul in the gut. Paul groaned as he doubled over. The hit sent him reeling backwards and down on the elaborate Persian rug.

Ben jumped on top of him. He was about to pummel Paul in the face. Abby cried out, "Ben—don't!" He froze, but just for a moment, then shoved Paul's head back to the floor.

He rose and made his way over to her. "Did he hurt you?"

She shuddered, but shook her head. "Please, get me out of here."

"So that's it, eh? You're with him now? Ha! Figures." Paul sat up, but he stayed put. "Wait until Preston hears about this. He's not going to like it one bit."

Abby turned to face him. "That should be about the same time he hears what you just attempted to do to me in here."

Paul's mouth opened to say something, but then he closed it without saying a word.

Satisfied she'd made her point, Abby took Ben's hand and walked out of the library.

She needed to get out of there.

She needed to get out of Maddy's hellacious life.

If only she could get back to the life she thought she had.

"Disgusting," Abby muttered under her breath as she and Ben stepped out of the limo and onto the sidewalk in front of Maddy's loft.

Ben followed her up the landing, to the front door. "Hey, it doesn't surprise me in the least that Paul is such a pig—"

"I wasn't talking about him—but yes, he's quite a son of a bitch, too." At the thought of him, she gave the hem of Maddy's tight skirt a modest yank, as if doing so might actually cover another half-inch of her thigh. Wishful thinking.

Ben tried not to notice. His smile proved otherwise.

Ignoring it, she put Maddy's key in the front door lock. "I meant Talbot. Did you see how he timed his departure so that everyone at the reception would take note of it? He didn't express his condolences to Uncle Preston. He gave a campaign speech! What was it he said? Oh yes: 'Andrew Mansfield was an American hero, and a worthy opponent.'"

"Yeah, the so-called mourners were tickled pink." Ben's laugh was devoid of humor. "History was being made, and they were a part of it. I counted at least twenty smart phones pointed at them.'"

Abby shrugged as she opened the front door.

Then she gasped.

The place was a shambles.

Ben put an index finger to his lips and motioned her to stay put. He grabbed one of Maddy's sculptures off the foyer table. It was only a foot long, but like all her pieces, rose to a sharp point. He held it like a weapon as he moved from room to room, then up the staircase to the loft.

No one.

He dropped the sculpture to his side.

His cell buzzed. The Caller ID came up as *Sukie*.

"The senator's townhouse was broken into, as were our campaign offices," she sobbed. "Everything's a mess. In the office, the files are all over the floor. And Andy's house has been tossed, too."

"I'm at Maddy's. They've done the same thing here."

"Who is 'they'?"

Ben could hear the fear in her voice. He knew he had to keep her calm, but keep her out of it, too. "Um...no one. Nothing. Don't...don't worry about it. Just—clean up as best you can. Call the private security firm that's supposed to be watching both places. Give them an earful. And have them send a three-man detail over here, too. Make sure they give us guards we know and trust." He sighed. "Sukie, you need to secure Andy's senate office, too."

"I'll call Security now, and tell them to beef things up."

As if that will keep them out, he thought as she hung up.

"What's happening?" Abby whispered.

"They think we have it." He plopped down on the couch. "Could your sister have hidden the envelope between the time she left me here, and when she met Andy at Manassas?" He rubbed his eyes, as if that could stir some hidden memory of those last few moments with her. "I got in my car and followed her, but only as far as the Roosevelt Memorial Bridge turn-off." He shrugged. "Wouldn't you know, it was the one time I needed to be obsessive about her, and I talked myself out of it."

"It takes less than an hour to get to Manassas," Abby reasoned. "Why would she have started the journey several hours prior to take-off? Unless she needed time to stop somewhere else—Oh my God! She detoured to Asquith Hall!"

"What? Would she have had time for that?"

Abby nodded. "Even in bad traffic, it's no more than two hours from the city. Afterward she could have easily circled back to Manassas."

He stood up. "I don't think we should waste any time."

She turned toward the window. "Do you think they're watching?"

"My guess is yes." He wished Maddy had curtains for the large open windows throughout the loft. "In any event, we can't let them see us leave."

Abby shivered. "Perhaps we should call the police. They can escort us out."

"Nope, not a great idea. If Fred has taught me anything, it's that we can't trust anyone. Who's to say that the real police would show up, anyway?" Watching her frown, he added, "Maddy's back staircase leads out into an alley. We'll leave the bedside lamp on, and nothing else. If they think we're staying put, we may just give them the slip. And besides, the security detail we use at campaign headquarters will be here momentarily."

He grabbed her arm and headed for the kitchen.

They went out the alley, and over to C Street, where they hailed a cab.

The tiny microphone left by Charlie, the Ghost op who had tossed the place, allowed him to hear their conversation. He cursed the fact that they didn't exactly spell out where they were headed.

He followed their cab to the Thrifty Car Rental office. Ben and Abby drove off the lot in a nondescript white Camry. This was reported to Smith, whose directive was just one word:

"Terminate."

Charlie got as far as Centreville, out on 66, before he lost them behind a tractor-trailer. Asquith Hall was nowhere to be found on his GPS.

The last thing he wanted to tell Smith was that they'd given him the slip.

It took him a couple of hours before he found someone who had heard of the place. When he asked a teenage clerk behind the counter of a Stop-N-Go in Gainesville, the kid gave him a shrug. Thankfully the old coot standing behind him overheard the question.

"That's the old Alcott homestead, just beyond Rixeyville. Follow 29, down through Warrenton. There, you'll pick up 229, which happens to be Rixeyville Road. Old Barn Road is on the left. You'll find Asquith Hall at the end of the road."

He thanked the man and the clerk with bullets to the head, then erased the store's video cam feed. No need for witnesses who might remember the man who asked about the estate, should the bodies of Ben Brinker and Maddy Vandergalen surface there.

He'd make sure they wouldn't.

Because if he fucked up, he'd be next on Smith's hit list.

CHAPTER 46

The road between the DC metroplex and Asquith Hall was not a well-traveled one. Ben found that comforting.

But he didn't really relax until they got onto Rixeyville Road. It was a just a two-laner, and it curved and flowed up and around the Northern Virginia hillsides. Every time he saw a pair of headlights in the rearview mirror, he sped up until he was sure the car behind him turned off.

By the time they reached Old Barn Road, he was bathed in sweat.

He was glad they got there after sundown.

Abby gave him the code that opened high wrought iron gates. A half a mile down the tree-lined drive, a three-story brick Colonial mansion loomed in front of them.

"It's dark. There's no staff on the property?"

"Not since Aunt Lavinia's bad fall last year. Uncle Preston insisted that she move into town. She now lives with him, in Georgetown." Abby frowned. "She hates it. At least, that's what she claims. But many of her life-long friends live there, too, and that has made things easier for her. She had a few of them with her today, at the funeral."

"Fred was among them."

"He was there?" Abby's eyes opened wide. "I didn't see him."

"You weren't supposed to. In fact, he was in drag."

Abby laughed. "Then I guess it's true that no one looks at an ugly woman. Shall we go in?" She practically ran to the front door.

She wants to get this over with as soon as possible. I can't say I blame her. Here's hoping we find what we came for.

The Alcott mansion was huge. Its common rooms were both large and high-ceilinged. Although the rooms contained a massive amount of ornate furniture, Ben and Abby's footsteps echoed as they made their way to the double staircase at the far end of the foyer.

Even with the lights on, the white sheets draped over the furnishings gave it a ghoulish feel.

The girls' bedrooms were the dormered rooms on the third floor. Inside, they could not have been more different. Abby's room had whitewashed pine furniture, and lace curtains on the windows. The bed was covered with a delicate quilt. The wallpaper had a floral pattern.

In stark contrast, graffiti had been scribbled on practically every inch of the gray walls in Maddy's old bedroom, and the furniture looked like thrift shop castoffs. Clothes and books were stacked all over the floor.

Ben's shock came out in a whistle. "Talk about angry. And I thought her sculptures made me queasy." He glanced around the room. "Where should we start?"

"Why don't you take the desk and the bed, and I'll take the closet?" Abby suggested.

When he slapped the old blanket on the bed, a cloud of dust rose to greet him. He reached under the bed, there was a stack of magazines—*Interview, Granta, Mother Jones, Rolling Stone.* He flipped through each copy in the hope that the envelope would fall out, but no luck.

The dresser held mostly jeans and old tee-shirts. He pulled each drawer out, in case she'd taped the envelope behind them, but he found nothing except a roll of old condoms.

That's my girl, he thought.

The top of the desk was also covered with a layer of dust. Still, he rummaged through the desk's drawers, which were filled with old school papers and a few pictures of heavy metal rock groups. Again, no envelope.

Frustrated he slammed one of the drawers, but it stuck. When he jerked it out again, a small book fell onto the floor.

It was sealed with a clasp. *Maddy's diary.*

Ben held it up to show Abby. "Would you mind if I take this with us?"

"I never even knew she kept a journal." Abby looked out from the closet. Her eyes were rimmed with tears. "I can't believe it. Half the clothes in here are similar to outfits I own. I guess she played my double on more than one occasion."

Ben frowned. He could only imagine Abby's pain at seeing the extent of her sister's duplicity. He wished he'd been the one to search the closet instead.

The hangers scraped across the rod with each angry stroke. "I've opened every box in here, and patted down all her clothes..." Abby's voice faded away. "Wait...there's a small door back here..."

He heard more rustling, then creaking boards. Finally Abby resurfaced. "Ben, is this the suitcase you saw at Maddy's place?"

It was bright red.

He nodded.

She swung it onto the bed. They both coughed as the dust flew up and hit them in the face. Ben unzipped the bag. Inside were the clothes he'd seen on Maddy the afternoon he confronted her at her apartment.

That day seemed so long ago. Without thinking, he patted Maddy's skirt. Emotions surged through him as the memory of taking her, there on the floor, came back to him.

He dropped his head in shame.

Abby laid her hand over his, but said nothing. When he finally looked up at her, he was touched by the concern in her eyes.

They stood there for what seemed like an eternity. Finally she murmured, "If you like, I'll check it for the envelope."

He nodded and stood back.

Abby lifted each piece of clothing from the suitcase. Nothing fell out. Three zippered pockets held a few cosmetics and nothing more.

Ben took a turn checking the outer surfaces for a hidden compartment, but none revealed itself.

"Another dead end," he muttered.

Abby sighed as she walked to the window. Looming under the galaxy of stars sprinkling overhead was Asquith Hall's tall box hedge maze. Suddenly she murmured, "Oh my God! How could I forget?"

Ben stared at her. "What is it?"

"Venus de Milo! In the hedge maze! It was our secret hiding place."

She was halfway down the stairs before he realized he should follow her.

Charlie found Asquith Hall with no problem. The old codger's directions were spot on.

The place was ablaze with lights. He wondered if they were

alone, or if there might be some collateral damage. Que sera, sera, what will be, will be. If so, he'd substitute the crazed campaign manager murder-suicide angle he'd been working on for a good old explosive fire with no known survivors.

An assassin was nothing if not flexible and resourceful.

He circled around the house, to get the lay of the land. Most of the ground floor windows were really French doors, or close to the floor in height. This allowed him to look inside the lit rooms on that level. There was no one to be seen.

He leaned back, better to scan all three levels of the house. The second story was dark, but the third floor dormer windows were lit up. Good. Knowing exactly where they were saved him from having to go room to room.

He came back around to the front of the house just in time to see the woman, Maddy, run out into the yard. The Brinker dude wasn't far behind her.

Here's the way the cops will see it: He let the bereft sis cry on his shoulder. When he got fresh, she ran out, and into that fucking garden maze. He followed, figuring he could rape her at gunpoint. They struggled, and he killed her instead. Not wanting to be some prison bad-ass's bitch, he put a bullet in his head.

Yeah, that'll work. From his back holster Charlie took out the drop gun he carried just for such an occasion.

This is going to be easier than he'd thought.

"Wait, Abby! Slow up!" Ben, who had been running to keep up with her, tripped over a root and landed on one knee.

He was groaning in pain when she reached him. She offered her hand to him. "I'm so sorry, Ben. Here let me help you up."

It was so dark that he could barely make her out. Her hand

sought out his, but it found his head first. Her fingers, brushing against his ear, made his heart beat that much faster. To calm it, he thought it best to focus on the task at hand. He grabbed her hand, but instead of pulling him off the ground, she fell on top of him.

With her chest against his, he realized her heart was racing, too.

Neither of them made a move.

Soon their hearts were beating in tandem.

He wondered what she was thinking about. Like his, was her mind churning over the events of the past forty-eight hours? Was she also scouring her memory for the telltale signs of the betrayal from those she loved most dearly?

Could she tell he cared for her?

My God, that's a hell of a loaded question, he thought.

But he couldn't deny it. Granted, her resemblance to Maddy had been the initial cause. Seeing her dressed like Maddy—acting like Maddy—aroused him to the point of shame.

No, make that guilt. He felt as if he were betraying his love for Maddy.

Had it been love, or merely lust? Wasn't love a mutually shared feeling?

Like Abby, Maddy had loved Andy. Ben could now admit that to himself.

He had not been able to save Maddy from herself, let alone from Andy's enemies.

But his feelings for Abby were more than just sexual attraction. He now knew he'd lay down his life for Abigail Jane Vandergalen Mansfield, if it came to that.

He prayed it wouldn't.

He also prayed the fact she hadn't stirred from his arms was proof that she felt the same way about him. When she put her finger on his lips, his heart skipped a beat—

Until she whispered in his ear, "*Shhhhh!* Did you hear that? Footsteps!"

He strained his ears until they detected the slow crunch of winter's dead leaves under the foot of the trespasser.

No doubt, it was the killer who had been sent to find them.

Or to torture them until they gave him the intel on Operation Flamingo.

She rolled off, but held fast to his hand, lifting him up with her, pulling him along side of her.

This time he had no problem keeping up.

If he had to, he'd follow her to the end of the Earth.

It was all coming back to her. *The third left. Then the second right. Now that you're at the three-way split, turn right again—*

Or should I take the middle path?

Abby stopped short. Ben wasn't expecting this, and almost pulled her arm out if its socket. She gave a small yelp.

She didn't mind at all when he pulled her close, or when he covered her mouth with his hand.

With him at her side, she was no longer scared.

She was determined to get out of this alive. She owed that to Maddy and Andy.

She owed it to Ben, who was risking his life for her.

"Which way do we go now?" he whispered.

"Both paths lead to the same place—the Venus de Milo statue, in the middle of the maze." To catch her breath, she gasped as she spoke. "But one of the paths was built over an old well. A few years ago the wooden boards covering the hole rotted away. It's directly in the middle of the path. I found it the last time I was out here, a few years ago, in broad daylight, of course. I mentioned it to Aunt Lavinia, but I know for a fact she never had it fixed because she hasn't walked through the maze in years, and thought it was a waste of money. She told me, 'You and Andy can do it when you inherit this old place.' It's dangerous. One false step and you'll drop at least thirty feet. But now I'm glad she held off, since it may save our lives."

"Or it might kill us first. How are we supposed to choose the best path, eenie meenie miney moe?"

She closed her eyes, trying to envision that day in her mind's eye. "It's....it's the one on the right."

Okay, then I'll go right and you go left. Walk slowly, so that he doesn't hear you. I'll be doing the opposite because I want to make sure he follows me. That way, at least one of us will get out of this alive."

"Please don't say that." She choked on her words. The thought of losing him, too, was too much for her.

"No matter what happens, get the file. Then get ahold of Fred. Call the CIA at Langley, and ask for him. His calls are being routed to a buddy. You're supposed to say something to the effect that his nephew Teddy's soccer game on Saturday has been postponed so no need to pick him up. Whoever answers will relay whatever you'll need to know in order to reach him."

No matter what happens...?

Of course, it mattered what happened to him! It mattered so much that her heart ached, just thinking about losing him—

"Abby," he hissed, "Did you get all that?"

She didn't say a word. Instead she lifted her head toward his and gave him a quick kiss on the cheek.

Then she ran down the left path.

Ben crawled up the path. For the most part he hugged the left side along the box hedge, as close as he could, but he swept his right hand out far along the ground, in search of the hole.

Another twenty paces later, he found it. In fact, he almost fell into it when the palm of his hand found nothing to brace it. He righted himself just in time. He felt around the edge of the hole until he was on the opposite side of the path's entryway.

There he waited, forcing his eyes to adjust to what little light there was. The thick tall hedges created a void that drank in all the starlight, except for the little that came from directly above him.

He coughed, and hoped whoever had followed them had good enough ears to hear it. As a precaution, he coughed again.

The footsteps were slow and so quiet that they seemed to come on the heels of the wind whistling through the hedge. Finally he saw the dark shadow of a man, his arms held high and together, bent at the elbow, holding a gun.

"Who the hell are you," Ben growled.

The man lowered the barrel of the gun and pointed it directly at Ben. "Step forward, hands held high." The man's command was accompanied by the click of the gun's trigger. "You and the woman. Where is she, by the way?"

Ben shrugged. "She went on ahead. I lost her."

"Maybe she'll find her way back if she hears you squealing like a piggy." Slowly the man walked forward.

Ben counted the steps—three...four...five...six...seven—until the killer was just two feet in front of the hole. Could he see it? Ben wondered. *Stall...just stall...* "Who are you? What do you want?"

The killer smirked. "Don't play dumb. We know you've got the envelope. I can make this very painful for you—and for the bimbo.

Go ahead and call to—"

His last word—*"her"*—echoed against the walls of the well as he fell to the bottom of it. Hearing the crunch of bone against brick drew Ben's eyes downward.

There were no other sounds.

When Ben looked up again, Abby was there, across from him, where the killer had once stood. "You...shoved him?"

"No. I gave him a sidekick. I have a black belt in kickboxing. Andy saw enough women get molested while he was in the service to insist I learn to protect myself." She stared down into the well, but saw nothing through the darkness.

"Abby, what you did was foolish! If he'd heard you come up behind him, he might have shot you—"

"If he'd heard me, you would have tried to save me. And maybe I'd be scolding you right now, instead of the other way around. Am I right?" She skirted around the hole and took Ben's hand. "We still aren't safe. The tables will turn again very soon, and you'll once again get my undying thanks. Until then, we'd better keep moving. Venus is waiting for us right around the corner." She nudged him forward. "I only wish we could have grabbed his gun before he fell."

He was thinking the exact same thing. Except he suspected that, of the two of them, she was a better shot.

CHAPTER 47

Asquith Hall's Venus de Milo was an exact replica of the original one, inside the Louvre. The center of the maze was also large enough to hold four benches, each facing the statue.

The statue's base was three-feet-square and made out of marble. Ben watched as Abby moved to the back of the statue. She crouched down beside the base's ornate moulding and tapped it hard, in the center.

The moulding popped off, revealing a space about two feet wide but the same height as the moulding—a mere three inches. Abby slid her hand into the space. With a slight smile, she pulled out what they were looking for:

An unlabeled manila envelope.

But the pages inside the envelope contained some undecipherable code. However, Fred taped a tiny, nearly flat, computer memory stick to one of them.

"Fred must have the password to open the files on this thumb drive," Abby murmured.

Ben nodded. "Halfway between here and DC, we'll do as he instructed and find someone to call Langley from a pay phone."

Abby shook her head. "We don't need to implicate anyone else who they might gun down. I'll make the call."

"No can do. The Ghost Squad may be monitoring calls to his extension, which I presume means it'll be put through some voice recognition software."

"Darlin', you jaist don't unnerstah-ann! Ah can disguise mah voice," she answered, in a syrupy Southern accent. Then in her own voice, she added, "Whenever his constituents were around, Andy laid it on thick. I guess it rubbed off."

He had to smile. "Okay, you're hired. Let's see if a phone booth still exists between here and DC."

They found one outside of a gas station, where Routes 29 and 55 intersected. He punched in the number, then handed her the receiver, which she held between them, so that he could listen in on the conversation.

Fred's line seemed to ring forever before someone picked up. It was a woman. After Abby asked for Fred Hanover, they heard a series of clicks before someone else came on the line. This time it was a man. "You wish to talk to Mr. Hanover?"

"Yes, thank you," Abby drawled sweetly.

"I'm sorry to be the one to inform you. Mr. Hanover died in an accident last night. His car skidded on some black ice, and jackknifed into the Potomac. They're dragging the river now. If you care to leave your name and number I can have someone call you with updates—"

Ben pulled the phone out of Abby's hand and hung it up.

She slumped against the gas station's cinderblock wall. "There must be someone else we can trust!"

Ben shook his head then stopped. Suddenly he grabbed the receiver and started dialing again. "Hey, Digits, it's me. Fred's dead, and I've got what he was looking for. At least, that's what they told me at Langley. Can we meet?...No, I'm calling from a phone booth. Yes, it's the same one....Oh, shit! I wasn't thinking...Where? Okay I—"

He stared at the dead receiver in his hand.

"What just happened?" Abby asked.

"I may have compromised the one guy who can decipher the message on this thumb drive."

She blinked away her tears. "So, now he won't meet with us?"

"He will, but we just can't walk into his place. And we've got to get out of here fast, in case the call was traced. In ten minutes, he'll be calling a phone booth at a convenience store, a mile down the road."

"Isn't he being a little paranoid?"

"He's got every right. Like Andy and Maddy, his father was a victim of Talbot's spy wars. Frankly, we couldn't have a better go-to guy. Even as we were talking, Digits pulled our location via the GPS tracker he tethered to his Caller ID, so whoever got to Fred could do the same to us." Ben looked over his shoulder. "All the more reason to get the hell out of here."

They walked back to the car in silence. He didn't have to tell her what they both already knew:

Their chances of staying alive were dwindling.

CHAPTER 48

They both had their ears to the pay phone as Digits explained his plan, which was this:

With cash only, they were to buy sun glasses, hats, scarves, jackets, magazines—whatever they needed in order to hide their faces from DC's many security cams.

Then they were to ditch the car in any free parking lot within walking distance to the Fort Totten Metro Rail Station. One would carry the thumb drive, while the other would hold onto the paper file. On the way to the station, they were to walk there on separate sides of the street, never acknowledging each other.

In fact, they were to enter the station from different sides, and buy their tickets separately. Abby would jump on the Red Line, and Ben would get on the Green/Yellow line, both southbound. The lines hooked up again at the Gallery Place/Chinatown Station.

"Why is he making us split up?" Abby asked.

"That's in case we're followed," Ben supposed. "They'll be looking for a man and a woman traveling together. If we separate and cover over our hair and eyes, they may not be able to ID us. And as it turns out, Fort Totten is the only station in which those three metro lines converge. If either of us picks up a tail, it'll be easier to lose them in there. As for Gallery Place, both the lines he suggested stop there as well, so eventually we end up in the same place."

Digits's directions then explained that they were to find the panhandling violinist who played in Gallery Place's ticketing lobby. If he played *Waltzing Matilda*, they should keep walking, and swap their train lines—he'd then jump on the Blue, while Abby would ride the Orange line—back in the direction they just came from, hook up again at L'Enfant, and get the hell out of dodge. However, if the violinist was playing *The Shadow of Your Smile*, Maddy should reach into the tip hat and leave a five dollar bill, and at the same time she'd pull out the tiny folded orange note, which would contain the directions to Digits's place.

If all went well, they were to rendezvous outside, across the street at the all night diner, taking the booth next to the back exit.

Should for any reason they get separated or feel they were being followed, they were to stay on the train beyond Gallery Place, to Metro Center, where they'd have the best chance of losing the tail, since it was the largest stop and serviced all four Metro lines. After losing their tail, they were to meet up again on the rooftop of the Momiji Lounge, on H at Fifth. A waitress named Laurel would give them a small envelope. They were to tip her well.

"Looks like he's thought of everything," Abby murmured.

Ben frowned. "Let's hope so. All our lives depend on it."

The Metro ride was uneventful. Ben was wearing cheaters and a baseball cap. He had exchanged his overcoat for a leather bomber jacket he bought at a Goodwill store next door for ten bucks.

He was the first to come upon the violinist in the Foggy Bottom station. Noting a security camera, he stood off to one side and pretended to read a copy of the *Washington Post*, which he'd salvaged from a bench.

He should have waited for Abby at the diner, but he already felt guilty for having left her unaccompanied since Fort Totten. He prayed she would make an appearance soon.

Six very long minutes later her train pulled into the station. She had purchased a navy raincoat, and had draped a black scarf over her head and shoulders. Her hair was tucked under it, so that no one could detect the color. She sauntered slowly, as if she didn't have a care in the world. When she reached the violinist, she stopped, as if entranced. When she dropped her five dollar bill, she bent slightly at the knee, which allowed her hand to disappear in the big bowler tip hat. He didn't see her pocket a note, but she put her hand in her pocket, so he guessed she had been successful.

Their eyes met for only a second. It seemed as though he'd learned to read the faintest glimmer of hope or shadow of fear that crossed her face.

He could tell she was feeling triumphant.

Ben waited a good five minutes after she was out of the station and had entered the diner before following her in.

It would be hard to keep from hugging her and never letting her go again, but he contained himself. In time, maybe she'd realize what she meant to him.

If they lived that long.

"Well, well, well, talk about the new year starting off with a bang." Digits's declaration was accompanied by a frown and a low whistle.

"Why? What are you looking at?"

"The biggest political hoax of all time." Digits looked up from his computer screen, where the file contained on the thumb drive was visible.

The directions on the orange note led Ben and Abby to a Chinese restaurant, where, as instructed, they ordered pot stickers, broccoli beef, and shrimp chow fun. With their order they were given a key. Further instructions, included in the bag, led them to an alley in back of the restaurant.

The key opened the back door. They took the rickety elevator to the fourth floor.

It opened up to a hallway containing just one door.

"Delivery," Abby shouted.

"About damn time," Digits said, as he opened the door. "Did they give you extra sweet and sour sauce?"

Abby didn't know what to say, but Ben did. "We're starved, so this better be for us."

Digits let them in. The room was immense. It took up the whole floor over the restaurant, but was also practically empty, except for a desk, a counter with a hot plate, a refrigerator, and a futon. The only light came from a dim desk lamp beside a laptop. Blackout curtains lined the windows that were on every side of the room.

He tossed Ben two sets of chopsticks. "Dig in while I break this puppy."

It had taken him about fifteen minutes to crack the password, but half an hour to break the encryption.

Abby was reading over his shoulder. "My God! Talbot will be faking a terrorist plot—on *New Year's Eve*?" She shook her head. "That's only seventy-two hours from now!"

"This gives us everything we need to take them down: schematics, even photos of the Venezuelan hostages who will be used as the human time bombs—"

"Aw, hell! The file contained a worm." Digits grabbed another memory stick and slid it into his computer. It was attached to a keychain fob with a Lara Croft image on it.

"A what?" Abby asked. "What does that mean?"

"It means you'll have to eat and run. Unfortunately the thumb drive contains some sort of tracker." He waited a moment, until the light on Lara Croft memory stick blinked green. He pulled it out and handed it to Ben. "I've scrubbed the intel and put it on this drive. Take it, along with the deciphered files, which are printing now."

As Abby reached over and pulled out the pages in the laser printer, Digits glanced out the window. "Aw, hell! Three cars just pulled up outside. Guess who's coming to dinner?"

With lightning speed, he ran to the refrigerator. Inside were a couple of cell phones and tall stacks of twenty-dollar bills, wrapped in cellophane.

He tossed Abby the cell phones and eight stacks of the cash, then grabbed a backpack and stuffed his computer into it before turning out the light. "This should be enough to get you out of DC. There's the fire escape on the back window. From there, you can jump onto the roof of the store next door. I'll be right behind you."

She was still cramming the stash into her purse as Ben pulled her out the window with him.

The ledge of the neighboring roof gave them a bird's eye view of six men in black, slipping silently up the staircase. The men had the door lock picked in no time. Apparently the lock to Digits's front door was also a breeze to jimmy because they yanked him back out, just as he was climbing onto the fire escape.

The men then walked out with Digits tossed over the shoulders of the largest of them.

"Oh my God!" Abby whispered. "Shouldn't we go back and help him?"

"If we do, they'll kill us, too." Ben slammed his fist against the wall. "Digits devoted his life to taking down the Ghost Squad. And Fred gave his life to see them brought to justice. We've got to get this intel to the right people."

"And who is that?"

"Hell if I know." Wearily, Ben slumped against the wall. "We've got to get out of here. Find a place to rest, if only for a few hours."

They waited until all three cars drove off before climbing down off the roof.

It was Abby's idea that they walk a few blocks to the National Theatre, where a show was letting out. "The crowd should be pretty thick. We can pick up a cab there, and take it to a hotel. We can sleep in short shifts. Maybe we'll dream our way out of this."

Ben nodded and stood up. With Fred gone and Digits in peril, he didn't have the heart to tell Abby that their chances of survival were now slim and none.

Smith would not have remembered Digits if, through the fog of pain that comes with all four molars being extracted without an anesthetic, the kid hadn't mentioned his father's little vacation in Hotel Transylvania.

He had to give Digits credit. It had taken one of Smith's spooks a full hour to knock his computer's security code out of him.

Finally the operative working Digits over asked, "I think we've gotten everything we can out of him. Should I put him out of his misery?"

Smith thought for a moment, but then an idea that came to him. "Nah. We're taking him with us to Vegas. That way, he'll be front and center for the Big Bang. This kid has been stateside all these years, so why not make it look as if he was the mastermind of Operation Flamingo? You know, like father, like son."

The operative shrugged.

Fucking numbnuts, thought Smith. He doesn't get it. Our job is theater. The huddled masses will eat it up. They love a good backstory.

His only disappointment was that they had once again let Ben Brinker and the bimbo slip through their fingers. But considering the pain therapy being administered, Smith had to believe Digits when he claimed he had no idea where they'd gone after they left him.

That was fine—for now. If they were running scared, it meant only one thing:

Any moment now, they'd reach out and trust someone they felt was safe.

The fools, he marveled. That's the point. You can't trust anyone.

They'll find that out soon enough.

CHAPTER 49

Ben would have preferred to take Abby to one of the nicer downtown hotels, but they couldn't take the chance of running into someone they knew, or that the hotels were being watched by Talbot's spies.

He opted instead for a shabby residential hotel just around the corner from the Greyhound bus depot on L and First, and paid for a full week in advance, cash. She waited outside while he paid cash for a room on the second floor and far in the back of the two-story cinderblock building.

The room was small. The furniture, made from a scarred wood-simulated melamine, was at least twenty years old. A thin blanket covered the lumpy double bed. An old television was bolted to a shelf high above the dresser.

"Home sweet home," Ben muttered.

"Tell you what, you take the first sleep shift," she insisted. "I'm too wound up to go to bed."

He was too, but he appreciated her offer. "I'm going to jump in the shower. Keep the door bolted and the chain on. And keep the curtains drawn, too. I'll make it quick."

Her nod was weak. She was obviously more tired than she cared to admit.

As he suspected, the water coming out of the corroded showerhead was tepid at best. Still, it felt great running down his back. He lathered up the best he could with the thin sliver of soap. There was no toothbrush. He wondered how bad his breath smelled.

Not that they'd had an opportunity to get up close and personal. They were both in mourning—of the lives they never really had.

When he came out of the bathroom, he found Abby curled up on the bed.

She'd been reading Maddy's diary, and she'd been crying.

He sat down beside her. "What's wrong?"

"All these years, Maddy had been suffering from such heartache, and I never suspected it." Abby tried to staunch her tears with the back of her hand. "That summer in New York, the man she was in love with—in the diary, she calls him 'Mr. X'—he took her virginity." She pointed to a passage, then flipped the page to another, and another, and another. "But Mr. X wasn't the only one. She had many lovers. They were all much older, and most were married. It was almost as if she was playing a game to see if she could somehow *make* them love her! She wrote that she knows nothing will come of it, as if she knew she was being used. After a while, she writes as if she's treating it like a blood sport."

Yes, that was the Maddy he knew.

"Here, hand me that." He motioned to the book.

Reluctantly she handed it over, as if she were afraid it might shatter his illusions of Maddy, too.

What she didn't know was that he no longer had any illusions about the one he once loved.

As he flipped through it, he came across a reference to a picnic. It stopped him cold.

"What's wrong?" Abby asked.

He shrugged. "I think you were wrong about how and when Maddy and Andy met. Listen to this. 'Firm picnic. Met THE ONE.

Tall, dark, handsome. Clerks for Atherton. What is it with Southern men? So polite, but a great flirt. Worth breaking date with X to find out.'"

Abby stared down at the bed. "I see. Is there anything else?"

Ben turned a few more pages, then stopped to read. "Ha...Yes, well, here she's nicknamed him 'my invisible man,' and adds 'but he hates it when I call him that. He doesn't understand why we can't be open about our relationship. I can't tell him about X. Not yet, anyway.'"

"I'd love to know who X was," Abby murmured.

"Yeah, you and me both." Ben leafed through the journal. "There are big gaps in the timeline. Sometimes she writes just a few words. 'Bliss.' Or 'We were almost caught—by X!'" He turned a few more pages before stopping. "Abby, you need to read this." He handed her the book.

X found out. Threw a fit, said it can't go on. I told him it would, and there was no way he could stop us. "I already have," he said. "He knows what will happen if he does." I told him to fuck off.

Took me three weeks to realize he was right. Andy wouldn't return my calls, so I went to the courthouse and cornered him. At first he refused to see me, but I told him I wouldn't leave until he did. That's when he told me it was all a big mistake.

Stupid, stupid me.

Abby turned the page. "All it says next is 'Being sent home.' The date of the entry matches the time in which she came back to Alquith Hall."

Ben picked up the book again. "The dates are blank, until the very last entry." He read it out loud:

That asshole, Paul! How could he have introduced Abby to Andy? And now, they're engaged?

I want to kill myself.

No. I want to kill X.

Abby grabbed the book from Ben. "Do you think X is Paul?"

"My guess is no. Otherwise she wouldn't have named Paul elsewhere in the journal."

"I guess you're right." She didn't sound convinced at all. "The date for this entry coincides with the date Andy and I announced our engagement. I told Maddy myself, over the phone. Now I know why she sounded so upset. I thought it was because she felt she might be losing me." She flipped a few more pages. "Want to hear the very last entry? It's dated the day after Andy was sworn in as senator." She picks up the journal with shaking hands. "She writes, 'He called. The Hay-Adams for cocktails, then the honeymoon suite. Bliss! My IM has come back to me.'"

IM.

Invisible Man.

She tossed the journal against the wall so hard that the spine broke. Loosened by the force, a few of the old journal's pages fluttered onto the floor.

Ben didn't blame her for being upset. "You're mad at Andy, aren't you?"

"Of course I am! He should have told me about them. Had I known, I would have never...I would have never fallen in love with him, let alone married him." She rose from the bed and paced the floor. "Why me? Why not Maddy? Was it for the money?"

"If money was his goal, both you and Maddy would have been equally desirable. That goes for the Vandergalen name and connections, too." What had Paul called Andy? Oh yeah: *the son of a pig farmer.*

"But he only chose me because I was the 'good twin'." The surge of anger now spent, she slumped back down on the bed and closed her eyes. "Maddy went out of her way to tweak the nose of the old guard. It made Uncle Preston furious. Her behavior burned lots of bridges, including the one Andy would have crossed, to be with her."

If he loved her, Andy would have been at her side despite what anyone thought, including Preston," Ben insisted.

I know I would have, he thought.

"Ah, you see? You don't know Andy any better than I did." She shook her head slowly. Despite the sarcasm in her tone, her voice sounded miles away. "He did this for the power. I was a silly little fool to believe it was anything else. Well, it backfired. Instead, he ruined all our lives. So much for love." Her voice drifted off.

He looked over at her. Despite her furrowed brow and her clenched fist, she seemed so helpless. He sat down beside her and patted her arm. The feel of her smooth skin stirred something in him. Not desire, as Maddy's touch had been capable of doing, but something deeper.

Bliss.

Overwhelmed by his emotions, he lay down beside her. The blanket had gathered on the other side her. As he reached over to pull it toward him, too, she sighed.

He fell asleep holding her.

Ben woke up with a start. He looked at the clock on the bedstand. He'd only been asleep a few hours. In fact, it was six in the morning.

Good. Rafe Lennox would already be in his office. The new chairman of the Democratic Party was always the first one through the door at the party's headquarters.

If anyone had a vested interest in breaking this story wide open, it was the opposition.

He grabbed one of Digits' untraceable cell phones and dialed the number he'd known by heart since he'd worked with his first candidate.

"Long time no see, you traitor," Rafe said, after hearing Ben's voice on the other end of the line. His tone was light and certainly a bit condescending. "I guess this call means the prodigal son is now looking homeward."

Ben didn't have time to play games. "I've got something I think you'll want to hear. In fact, I'd suggest Bradley Cridge, Reuben Edelson, and Edgar Concha should also be in on this. I can be in your office in one hour."

"I presume you'll make it worth our while?" Of course Rafe would ask that, considering that Ben had just asked that the Democratic Senate and House leaders, as well as the chairman of the Senate Committee on Homeland Security and Governmental Affairs, be in attendance.

"You'll have to trust me. The repercussions will affect the party for years to come."

Ben's tone was all it took to convince Rafe. "I'll tell Security not to toss you out on your ass when you get here."

Ben left a note for Abby: *Stay here. Keep the door locked, and the Do Not Disturb sign on the knob. I'll bring food. Promise.*

He had to stop himself from also writing that should anything go wrong, he hoped she knew he had a tremendous respect and love for her.

If he came back, he'd tell her that in person.

CHAPTER 50

As Ben laid out his story from beginning to end, he watched the expressions on the faces of Democratic Party leaders change from annoyed, to intrigued, to incredulous—

And then to wary.

Ben looked from one man to the other. "Look, I know it sounds far-fetched. One GOP presidential candidate is blown up by another, who also happens to be the sitting Vice President. To top it off, this nut job wants to blow up Las Vegas and pin it on an oil-rich country. It's certainly a conspiracy theorist's wet dream."

No one said a word.

"Here, in case you need a visual aid." He pulled the printed files they'd taken from Digits's place, and spread them out on the massive conference table.

Gingerly the men picked through them. Ben watched the shock and awe on their faces as they sifted through the schematic that laid out the who, what, where, when and how exactly as it would play out: the photos of the supposed terrorists; the purchase of a ranch where a private hell had been built for them; even where the human bombs would be standing when the clock struck midnight.

The men's eyes shifted from one to another. Finally Rafe spoke. "Listen, Ben, as tempting as it would be to knock the GOP presidential frontrunner on his ass prior to the election—

particularly with a scandal involving treason—how do we know this stuff is legit?"

Ben smacked the table. "You didn't just land in DC. For Christ's sake, for years the rumors have been circulating about Talbot's Ghost Squad—"

"That's just it," Senator Cridge cut in. "It's just a rumor. No one's been able to verify it."

Exasperated, Ben ran his hand through his hair. "Then send someone out to the ranch, to check it out. Find out who yanked those illegals off from immigration. Go to Digits' apartment to—"

Congressman Edelson shrugged. "And we're supposed to do this within the next sixty-eight hours?"

"Yes, Congressman! Party posturing aside, another part of your jobs is to prevent a terrorist attack on US soil! Thus far three men and one woman have given their lives, because they stood in the way of this scheme of Talbot's. Gentlemen, the clock is ticking, so get your dicks out of your hands and do something."

"That's uncalled for, Mr. Brinker." Senator Concha growled. "For that matter, how do we know this—this preposterous accusation isn't just something you cooked up to fool us into making scurrilous accusations against the GOP frontrunner? If this crap is faked, we'll look as if we've been duped by forgers. Or worse, we'll be perceived as dirty tricksters ourselves." His eyes narrowed as he leaned back. "Come clean. How much did Talbot pay you to slip this steaming bowl of shit our way, so he can watch us eat it in front of the press and the American public? Sucking on one GOP tit is no different from sucking on another, am I right?"

Ben couldn't believe his ears. It suddenly dawned on him, either they're too stupid to see the importance of stopping Operation Flamingo, or they're too scared.

"Look Ben, you've got to admit that all of this does sound somewhat...well, *fantastical*. Considering the shock you've gone through, what with losing Mansfield and all, maybe it's time to take a breather, a little vacation." The tone in Rafe's voice was meant for a six-year-old who was refusing to eat his vegetables, certainly not respectful of someone who had won every race he'd ever managed for these sons of bitches.

Enough of this shit, Ben thought. I guess my next stop is the *Post.*

"Gentlemen, your collective lack of courage is disappointing, to say the least. Come New Year's Eve, should Operation Flamingo take place, that footnote in history you all so desperately covet will finally be yours. Granted, you won't like how it reads, but then again, cowards rarely do."

Plucking the thumb drive out of Rafe's hand, he scooped the pages off the table and headed out the door.

Smith had learned it was just as prudent to have friends in low places as to have them in the highest echelons of power.

There was no place lower than the bulk supply store used by the DNC, where it purchased everything it needed: pens, pads, staplers, and even American flag lapel pins for its Congressional members.

In fact, as pleased as the DNC's purchasing assistant was with the enormous discount Smith had arranged for her, she was gaga over its exclusive design. Besides being four-color cloisonné and 14-carat gold rimmed, the pins contained tiny microphones, which were monitored by Smith's ghosts.

No doubt about it, the Dems' cheeky foibles kept his men in stitches. And every now and then, the mics dropped a solid gold sound bite right in Smith's lap.

Like now, when Ben Brinker's whereabouts were revealed, along with Senator Cridge's obvious heart murmur.

But of course Brinker would have run to his old Dem buddies, Smith reasoned. And of course even if they'd found the accusation against Talbot believable, they'd deem it too hot to handle. Cridge, Edelson and Concha were only living up to their nicknames: See No Evil, Hear No Evil, and Speak No Evil.

The only balls in the Sheeple's Party could be found between the legs of the Party's Congressional Majority Leader—who just so happened to be a woman.

Smith sent two ghosts to pick up Brinker.

He also sent a text to Talbot suggesting that the GOP line up a strong candidate for Cridge's seat, now that it seemed that the portly fellow wasn't long for this world.

As he suspected, the Veep wrote back, asking if this untimely demise could take place, say, maybe a week prior to the absentee ballots going out.

Smith texted back: *Miracles do happen.*

Then he put it on his calendar.

He loved planning October surprises.

Norm Phister, proprietor of the Two Bits, the busiest shoeshine stand in the Capitol South Metro Station, was a guy who kept his head down. But that didn't stop him from keeping his wits about him. "Ben, ol' boy, you know you're being followed, right?" he murmured as he wiped down Ben's chocolate brown Bally derbies. "Man, these shoes have been through hell—"

Ben shifted his newspaper so that he could look down at Norm without being seen from passersby. "Where are they?"

Norm didn't even look up. "The tall drink of water on your left, and the broad shouldered short guy, slightly to the right, who keeps looking at his watch. Don't look up now, or they'll know you're onto them. More than likely CIA. Look hard and you'll see the ear buds."

Ben nodded slightly. "I've got to leave something behind. Can you hold onto it for me? I'll make it worth your while."

"For fifteen years I've been buffing your brogues. I'd say you've already paid off handsomely. That said, a five-star Yelp review wouldn't hurt."

"Consider it done." Ben could have added *If I survive this,* but kept his mouth shut. "It's a thumb drive. I'll hand it over with a twenty. Put it somewhere safe, Norm. Many lives depend on it. I'm headed to the *Post.* Unless I, or a reporter with a specific codeword—'waypoint'—shows up to collect it, hold onto it for dear life."

Norm brushed the toe of Ben's right shoe. "Then you better make the next Orange Line. It'll be here in exactly fifteen seconds."

"Thanks," Ben muttered. Then, as he jumped out of his chair, he said in a normal voice, "Looks great, guy! Here, keep the change."

Ben's generous tip earned him a hardy handshake.

The ghosts were too busy hopping onto the same train car as Ben to notice the shoeshine man's lightning speed sleight of hand as he slipped the thumb drive into the polish tin farthest from the right on the lowest shelf of his shoe shine stand. Although marked POLISH - WHITE PATENT LEATHER. The polish was long gone, and had been, for many years.

To Norm's disappointment, go-go boots weren't making a comeback anytime soon. At least his nostalgia paid off for Ben.

There were six stops between the South Capitol Metro and the

McPherson Square stations. Ben saw the two men. Both were dressed in suits, like most of the other downtown commuters, but their earpieces were the giveaway.

Despite it being the week between Christmas and New Year's, the platform was crowded. When the train stopped, everyone surged forward, including Ben.

Unfortunately, his stalkers were right behind him.

For that matter, they were too close for comfort—almost within arm's length.

He went for the door farthest to the right in the hope of scrambling onto another car at the very last second, but the number of passengers hopping off made it an impossible feat. He had nowhere to go but into the car, with his stalkers on his heels.

The car was jammed so tightly that it seemed natural for the men to stand directly behind him. So close, that they could breathe on his neck.

So close that one of them easily injected him with some drug.

He seemed to freeze in place, unable to shout, to move, to warn the other passengers staring off into space that their placid lives would soon change forever unless they could read the fear in his eyes and help him escape from his captors. But avoiding eye contact in mass transit is a skill that has been honed by too many, Ben among them.

Had he been a crazy man, shouting about bombs and terrorists, would someone had come to his aid? No. The subway cops would have leaped on him.

And eventually, Smith and his men would have been summoned to take him away.

At the next stop, each of the men grabbed an arm and led him off the train.

He knew his next stop was Hell.

CHAPTER 51

By four o'clock that afternoon, Abby had paced the room so many times that she could have walked to Baltimore and back again. Where was Ben? Why hadn't he called?

What if he were dead?

I can't stay here forever, she reasoned. I have to get out of here...

But where can I go?

Deep down in her heart, she knew there was only one person who would understand, who could ensure their safety:

Uncle Preston.

She grabbed her purse, left the DO NOT DISTURB sign on the outside knob, and locked the door behind her.

"My dear, you're hugging me so hard, I'm sure I can hear my bones crack." Aunt Lavinia's chiding was all in jest. In truth, it was the older woman who held onto her niece, as if she would never let go.

Abby didn't mind at all. She too laughed, through a scrim of bittersweet tears.

"Speaking of bones, you are much too thin these days," Aunt

Lavinia muttered. "I know it's because you're upset. And your heart is broken. You've lost the dearest person in the world to you: your sister." Lavinia squeezed her hand firmly. "And your husband."

My God, she knows I'm Abigail.

Abby raised her head in order to look her aunt squarely in the eye. "How did you know?"

"You and Maddy may have looked like two peas in a pod, but to me, you've always been as different as night and day." A thin smile lifted Lavinia's lips slightly at their corners.

"Does Uncle Preston know, too?"

Lavinia's eyes grew large. She was just about to speak when they heard the front door open.

The steps coming in their direction were slow, but strong. A moment later, Uncle Preston appeared in the living room entrance. Seeing his niece, he seemed genuinely relieved. "My dear girl! I've been so worried about you! Where have you been? Why haven't you answered your cell phone?"

Before she could respond, he added, "Lavinia, if you don't mind too terribly, I must have a private word with Maddy."

Ah, so Lavinia never told him what she suspected, Abby realized.

Before Abby could say a word, Lavinia leaned in to kiss her. While doing so, she whispered, "No. Not yet."

But...why not?

Abby watched, perplexed, as her aunt made her way to the door, shutting it behind her.

Uncle Preston put his arm around her. "My dear, I realize these events have put you in such a delicate state." He smiled broadly. "And I know Abby and Andy's estates are merely the consolation prize. But I hope it gives you some comfort to know that, with their combined assets at your disposal, you'll never want for anything."

What the hell is he talking about?

"I'm sorry, Uncle Preston," Abby stuttered, "I don't understand..."

He held her hands as he drew her down on the settee with him. "Odd. I would have thought Andy had mentioned it to you. Of course he named you as his benefactor, should Abby predecease you."

More proof that he had stayed in love with Maddy, even after his marrying me, Abby thought sadly.

"Buck up, darling. It's the least you deserve, having kept him happy, all these years. Your discretion was truly the greatest part of valor."

So, he knew of their affair—

And he approved of it.

She was so shocked at this revelation that she sunk back into the settee.

The next thing she knew, her uncle's lips were on hers—

Disgusted, she shoved him away. "My God! What do you think you're doing?"

Despite his obvious annoyance, Preston laughed. "Don't play coy, Maddy. I'm trying to comfort you." His smile disappeared. "When Andrew was alive, you made it quite clear you weren't going to be shared, and I honored your decision. But now that he's gone, I presumed you'd want our relationship to pick up where we left off—"

"How...*disgusting!*" Abby stood up. "All these years...It was you! You're the reason why she changed, why she was so sad, so jaded—why she resented me, all these years!"

"Calm down! Lavinia might hear you!" In a second he was beside her. He twisted her arm, then he jerked it up behind her back until the excruciating pain had her bending to his will, over the arm of the settee. "Who the hell are you talking about?" he hissed in her ear.

Her silence earned her another painful jerk. Finally she gasped, "Maddy, you deplorable sadist!"

The shock of her declaration caused him to loosen his grip for just a moment.

It was long enough for her to turn around and slap him.

Angrily he punched her in the gut. As she doubled over, he shoved her back down onto the settee. "Abigail?...Why, you silly little fool! Let me guess: it was Brinker's idea that you transform yourself into the tart. Figures. He's so obsessed with her." Preston placed his hand between her legs. At the same time his fingers inched up her thighs, the bile rose in her throat. "Has it been fun, playing the harlot? Has your grief so overwhelmed you that you let him have you?"

His hand found her panties. She felt his finger coil around and yank them down. "If you can be his Maddy, you can be mine, too—"

Her fist found its mark. The pain in his kidney weakened him enough that she could get out from under him.

Still aching from his punch, she stumbled to the door.

He threw out his foot and tripped her.

As she fell onto the parquet floor, she banged her head against the marble coffee table.

She was too groggy to understand all he was saying to her. But no, he was talking to someone else, on the phone. She heard him say something about having someone take her to Maddy's loft...Ben's DNA...Sordid sex play...and lovers found dead in a murder-suicide...

So they have Ben, too.

Poor, sweet, brave Ben.

She felt Preston's lips upon hers again, and heard him

whisper, "Once again, the wrong twin was in the wrong place at the wrong time. What a shame."

Yes, what a damn shame.

Before she blacked out, her last thought was *At least I'll die in Ben's arms.*

This gave her some comfort.

CHAPTER 52

The only thing good about Ben being awake while Talbot's Ghost Squad took him to their torture chamber was that he could at least identify where it was—some old millworks that squatted on the banks of the Potomac.

The worst thing about it was the amount of pain he had to endure as they punched him black and blue before taking a pair of pliers and ripping two nails from the fingers on his left hand.

Ben groaned, but he refused to give them the satisfaction of screaming.

Smith sat in a corner, reading a *New Yorker*. Every now and then he'd look up, but he was obviously disappointed that Ben wasn't giving him more of a show. "Go ahead," he nudged. "Yell all you want. No one can hear you here."

"He's a stubborn motherfucker, boss," the short one said.

"We could always 'board him, boss, like his little Venezuelan buddy," the taller of the two ghosts added. "Then we can drown him. Ooops!"

The Shorty one guffawed at that, but not Smith. He rose and walked over to Ben. From his pocket he pulled out a gun. It was small, and seemed to be made of sterling silver. The handle was covered with ornate embossing.

He held it in front of Ben's face. "Beautiful scrollwork, isn't it? Made in the 1930s, in Japan. They don't make them like this anymore."

Smith lowered the barrel until it was pointed at the bridge of Ben's nose. When he pulled the trigger, Ben closed his eyes—

Only to hear a soft *whoosh.*

Ben opened one eye. A flame glowed and swayed on top of the gun's barrel.

Smith laughed uproariously. His thugs joined in. When finally they quieted down, he took the envelope containing the printed intel, and lit it on fire. "*Ah,* I love the smell of butane in the morning," Smith murmured.

Ben winced as he watched it burn. The ashes wafted gently in a draft blowing in through a broken window pane before floating to the concrete floor.

Smith grabbed Ben's hand and flipped it over, palm down. Then he yanked one of Ben's bleeding fingers—the middle one— directly over the flame. When a droplet of blood hit the flame, it flared and sizzled.

The sound of it was as nauseating as the heat on the finger's exposed nerve endings.

But not as painful. Smith nodded to his men. One slammed his wrist down on the table so that his hand hung over the edge. The other grabbed his fingers so that he couldn't make a fist.

Smith held the flame of the lighter under his palm.

Instinctively Ben tried to yank his hand away from the heat, but the men held on tight.

"You know what they say," Smith said, "You play with fire, you get burned. Now, tell me: where's the thumb drive you showed those chicken shit DNC yutzes?"

"I...I left it with them." Ben gagged at the smell of his own burning flesh.

"Don't bullshit me. We've had their conference room bugged for over a year now. We know they were too stupid to take it. So, where is it?"

"When I saw your goons here were trailing me, I dropped it on the floor of the train when I jumped onto the Orange Line. I swear!" Ben's words came out in pained gasps. "I thought they were just going to roll me. You know, lift the papers and run off at the next stop. I was going to grab it off the floor after they took off—"

Smith held the flame steady.

The tears rolled down Ben's face as the heat seared his palm.

Finally Smith lowered the flame. "If what you say is true, you're even stupider than you look. But unlike your Spic pal, I've got no reason to take you along on our little Vegas junket."

Digits was still alive after all...

For now, anyway.

"I guess this is the end of the line for you." He snapped his fingers at the other men. "Make it look like he went in for a swim but forgot how to dog paddle."

Shorty slapped electrical tape over Ben's mouth and his wrists while Too Tall yanked Ben to his feet. They were both dragging him, kicking, toward the door when Smith's cell phone rang.

The conversation was short and sweet—nothing Ben could hear, even if he had tried to listen instead of struggling to get out of their grip.

"Change of plan, boys," Smith called out. "We've got the woman, too. Al's holding her at her place."

Ben groaned. Why hadn't Abby stayed put?

"Make it look like they had too much fun. You know, like he choked her to death or something, then felt guilty about it and blew his brains out." The thought of it made Smith's lips widen into a blissful smirk.

Too Tall furrowed his brow. "Is she into kink?"

Smith sighed. "How the hell would I know? Okay, from the

looks of her, maybe. But don't presume anything. Stop off at the Pleasure Palace on Wisconsin. If they don't have what you need, improvise. There's a Home Depot down the block." He started out the door. "I've got a plane to catch. Text me after the extermination."

He looks like the skull on the poison bottle, Ben thought as the door slammed shut behind him.

Shorty shouldn't have bent down to tie his shoe.

The metal bat came down so fast and so hard on his skull that he didn't have time to scream.

Like Ben, Too Tall heard what sounded like a sack of potatoes hitting the asphalt. Instinctively he turned around to assess the situation. When he did, the bat cracked his nose like glass. But before he could scream, it slammed into his gut.

As he collapsed to the ground, the air went out of him, like a balloon with a slow leak.

Ben tried to scramble away, but was jerked back onto his feet—

By Fred.

"They told me your car went into the Potomac!" Ben gasped.

"It did. Unfortunately, it can't swim, but I can." Fred smiled broadly. "Here, help me put these guys in the trunk in case Smith comes back before we have a chance to get the hell out of here."

"Smith? That's his name? Not so original." Ben grabbed Too Tall by the chest and dragged him to the back of the car. But before shoving him into the trunk, he scooped the man's cell phone out of his pocket and tossed it to Fred. "Smith told him to text after the 'extermination'." The word sent a shiver up Ben's spine.

Fred trotted over to Shorty, heaved him over his shoulder, then walked back to the trunk and tossed him in as well.

Ben jumped into the passenger seat. Despite the throbbing pain in his hand, he felt elated. He would have hugged Fred if he wasn't afraid his friend would drive into a pole.

Or punch him.

Then he remembered Abby.

"Fred, they've got Abby! They're holding her at Maddy's place—"

Fred stared at him. "You mean, that wasn't Maddy at the funeral?"

Ben shook his head. "It was Maddy who....who died with Andy. They were having an affair."

Fred didn't say a word.

Ben slumped down. "You knew, then."

"Not exactly. I knew they were an item, years before his marriage." He shrugged. "Just before I met Abby, Andy swore me to secrecy. He told me that what was in the past was just that: old news, history. He didn't want to cause a rift between the sisters. He told me Maddy wanted it that way, too. She tried not to show it, but anyone who'd known them before could see it." Fred hesitated. "I presume Abby knows, too?"

"Yes. She took it pretty hard. She loved both of them, so of course it was quite a shock." Ben frowned. "They're holding her, at Maddy's place. These goons were supposed to take me there, so that they could stage a murder-suicide."

"If we had time, we could do the same to them. They'd make quite a tableau."

"We don't. At least, not according to the plans you downloaded onto the thumb drive. Operation Flamingo is set to go off in Las Vegas, New Year's Eve, just as the clock strikes midnight."

"So, Digits was able to decipher the damn thing?"

"Yes—and just in time, too. Abby and I escaped with it, but unfortunately they got him. Smith mentioned they'll be planting Digits right in the middle of Operation Flamingo."

"Not if I can help it." Fred turned onto Dupont Circle. "So where is it now?"

"With Norm, at the Two Bits Shoe Shine stand, in the South Capitol Metro Station." Ben turned to face him. "How did you come across the intel?"

Fred shook his head. "I don't like to divulge my sources." He pulled over to the curb. "We're here."

Ben looked out the window. "No, we're not! This is some pizza joint."

"No, it's not just 'some pizza joint.' It's *Pizzaria Paradiso*. The best in Dupont Circle. I've already ordered a Siciliano, a couple of bottles of beer, and one of their signature caps. While you're making the delivery at the front door, I'll enter through the back."

"You'll find the key over the door ledge." The memory of Maddy jibing him about hidden spare keys came back to him. It seemed like a million years ago.

Tell whoever answers it was paid for in advance, and be sure to give the guy some shit about your tip. That'll give me time to make my move."

"You've thought of everything, haven't you?"

"Let's hope so. By the way, I hope you like eggplant."

CHAPTER 53

At first, the ghost wouldn't open the front door.

And yet, he was right here, just on the other side.

Ben hadn't heard his footsteps but he had tuned his ear to the creak of the loft's floorboards.

The last one stopped right in front of the door.

There was no light coming through the peephole.

Smith's ghost was right there, on the other side.

What had taken him so long? What had he been doing to Abby?

Ben banged frantically on the door. He rang the bell, over and over. He slammed his fist on the door, as hard as he could. "Dude, you bitch when we don't deliver hot, and we live to please, remember?" he shouted, desperately. "I don't want you pissed at me, like last time, for leaving before you got off the john...or whatever—"

The door opened, but only as far as the security chain allowed. The man on the other side of it—bulky, mid-height, with curly hair—stared out at Ben. "Fuck off."

Ben tried hard to smile. "A large Siciliano and two beers. You already paid for it. You might as well take it, right?"

He prayed the bead of sweat rolling down his forehead would get sopped up by the *Pizzeria Paradiso* cap before rolling down his nose.

The man's eyes narrowed. He shrugged and shut the door.

If Ben had been quicker, he would have stuck his foot in the door and barged his way in.

He didn't need to. The thought of free pizza and beer must have gotten the better of Smith's man because a moment later the door opened wide, freed from the chain that kept Ben from Abby.

But before Ben could take a step forward, the man positioned himself in the center of doorway and held out his hands.

Ben smiled and handed him the pizza box, but out of the corner of his eye he watched as Fred inched his way out of the kitchen.

As if sensing Ben's distraction, the man's eyes turned slightly.

"No anchovies, and pecorino, just like you asked," Ben murmured with a smile. "We were out of Anchor Liberty, so we upgraded you to Avery Out of Bounds Stout. Is that okay?"

The man gave him a wary nod. "Yeah. Now, fuck off."

"Well, you know we live on our tips—"

The man shoved the pizza box into Ben's chest. "Oh yeah? Well, here's a tip. Get lost before I cram one of these bottles up your ass—"

Ben shoved back.

Bad move. Fred's shot, aimed for the guy's head, hit the door frame instead.

When the man rolled out of the fall, he had a gun in his hand. His first shot winged Fred's shoulder. Fred groaned and jumped back into the kitchen.

He then turned toward Ben, who had leaped over the high-backed couch. He yanked the table lamp onto the floor with him, so that the only light in the room was coming from where it had landed, illuminating Maddy's sculptures upward so that they loomed out of the shadows. Their sharp points appeared to have tripled in size.

Two of her metal statues also fell. One—just a foot long, with a small square base that rose to a sharp point—barely missed his head, piercing a throw pillow instead. Ben prayed the man didn't see the cloud of downy feathers rising around him.

He needs me, she thought. Just like I need him.

She'd passed out when she'd fallen against Preston's coffee table. When she came to, she found herself in Maddy's bed, naked. A strange man had just finished tying her, spread-eagled, to the bedposts with silk stockings that must have belonged to Maddy.

"You've got quite a collection of whore couture," he said with a smile. He leaned in so close that she smelled cigarettes on his breath. When he hefted one of her breasts in his hand and tweaked it between his thumb and forefinger, she shuddered despite the fact his hands were gloved. "I'd take a go at you myself, but I'm only allowed to fondle the merchandise. Can't leave any DNA around, you know."

She spit in his eye.

Angered, his arm went back. He was just about to backhand her across the face when the doorbell rang.

At first he froze. Then he took another stocking and wrapped it over her mouth. He yanked it so tight that she almost gagged. "I guess my buddies are here with your boyfriend. When I get back, we'll have a little fun with this dildo collection of yours. We're going to make it look like your sweetheart got a little out of hand." He yanked open the bedstand drawer.

Abby looked down, then turned away.

He laughed as he ran down the stairs.

I've got to get out of here, she thought. She strained against her bindings, but they held tight. Panicked, she twisted her wrists and kicked her legs.

The voices below were getting louder, more anxious. She recognized one as Ben's—

Then she heard the gun shots.

He's outnumbered. I've got to help him, she vowed.

Because he can't die. I don't know what I'd do if he died.

I couldn't live without him.

Because I...

I love him.

That realization set her free, right then and there, from Maddy and Andy's ghosts.

Freed from her anger, and her jealousy.

She forgave them for loving each other more than they'd loved her.

Ben loved her. She saw it in the way he looked at her. And she knew it from the way he looked after her.

He was willing to make the ultimate sacrifice for her.

Just as Maddy had made the ultimate sacrifice for Andy.

At least they were together at the very end, Abby reasoned. And Ben will be with me.

But it will not end this way for us. Not if I can help it.

She struggled with all her might. Suddenly she noticed that the stocking around her right wrist had snagged itself on one of the metal finials on the headboard. She jerked it as hard as she could—

Until it ripped.

Quickly she untangled her hand from the stocking, then untied her other hand and her feet, and shot out of the bed. She looked around for something to throw at her assailant, anything at all—

The mirror.

It hung over Maddy's vanity. Despite its heft and bulk, she lifted it off the wall. It could shield her from bullets, if it came to that.

If she couldn't protect Ben, she'd die trying.

She ran to the loft railing with the mirror, and looked down.

"Come out, come out, wherever you are, Pizza Boy," Smith's man declared as he circled the room.

From there on the floor Ben could look out between the couch legs. It took a moment for his eyes to adjust to the shadows.

The only one moving belonged to Smith's man.

He hadn't thrown a javelin since his high school track and field days. Even back then, his aim was usually shaky enough that the spear wavered when airborne and rarely hit the designated target, sailing right past it instead.

This time, though, he couldn't afford to miss.

Not with Abby, now naked and carrying a huge wall mirror and staring down at him from the balcony.

Her shadow also caught the attention of Smith's man. He turned and swung his gun up and around, but he hesitated when he saw his own reflection staring down at him.

Ben realized this was his chance. He leaped up. Grabbing the sculpture, he yelled, "Beer coming your way!"

When the man turned to face him, Ben hurled the pointed sculpture as hard as he could.

Smith's man gasped when it stabbed him in the gut.

As he toppled backward, the gun dropped out of his hand.

Abby threw down the mirror and ran down the stairs, into Ben's arms.

It suddenly dawned on her that she was still naked, but that didn't stop her lips from seeking out his or from covering his face, his neck, his chest, with her kisses as she sobbed.

"Bullseye." They were interrupted by Fred's faint croak. He was crouching on the floor and breathing heavy.

Together Abby and Ben lifted him up. "Pick up the gun," he muttered to Abby. "And while you're at it, you might want to put on some clothes. Oh yeah, and grab the pizza on the way out."

They let him eat it on the way to some doctor he had on call for, as he put it, "little incidents like this." Remembering Ben's remark about Smith, he took Too Tall's cell phone out of his pocket. Smith's ID was, simply, Boss.

Fred texted *PROBLEM SOLVED*.

"I guess that buys us a little time," Ben said.

Wishful thinking, each of them thought, but no one dared to say it out loud.

CHAPTER 54

The lunchtime line at Pete's Carry-Out was moving pretty quickly. Too quickly in fact, for Ben. He glanced down at his watch for the umpteenth time, wondering what was taking Norm so long to get there, when the man behind him growled, "How's the egg salad in this joint?"

Ben heaved a sigh of relief at the sound of his friend's voice. "Word of warning: too much mayo."

Norm chuckled. "I'll take that as the password that the coast is clear."

Ben felt something drop into his right coat pocket. He glanced around the room to see if anyone had been watching, but no. The thick crowd seemed preoccupied bantering with their lunch partners, or else they were perusing their smart phones.

Will my life ever be normal again? Ben wondered.

Ben slipped his hand into his pocket, where he found a round tin. He shook it gently. The rattle of the thumb drive was music to his ears.

He nodded his thanks before jumping out of the line and making for the door.

It was Fred's idea that they grab one of the tall booths at Chief

Ike's Mambo Room to confab on what to do next. He knew for a fact that it (a) wasn't a spook or government wonk hangout, and (b) there were no security cameras.

In fact, Ike growled if he saw a smart phone on the premises. What happened in the Mambo Room stayed in the Mambo Room.

Abby downed a whisky as she broke the news to Ben about her encounter with her uncle.

"Preston is in on it, too?" Ben's hands curled into fists. No wonder Maddy was so wounded.

So, Preston Alcott was X.

"Yes," Abby and Fred said at the same time.

Ben and Abby stared at Fred. In unison, they asked, "How long have you known?"

Fred shrugged. "Since Lavinia handed me the thumb drive."

"You mean—she's your source?" Abby and Ben asked at the same time.

Fred threw up his hands. "What is this, a vaudeville act?" Old habits are hard to break. His eyes darted in all directions as he murmured, "Lavinia and I met at your wedding, Abby. She felt I had the right sort of job to investigate her suspicions. One day she overheard Talbot and Preston going over the fine points of Flamingo. Your uncle was angry. He thought it was too risky, but he signed on."

Hearing this, Abby downed the last sip in her whisky glass. Ben did the same. It just gets better, he thought wryly.

"Lavinia was angry at her brother. The Alcotts fought in Washington's army. Abby, as you're well aware, your father's folk, the Vandergalens, were among New York's first settlers. The day of Andy and Maddy's trip, Preston was on one of his New York junkets. Lavinia allowed me into his private study. The files on the thumb drive were downloaded from his computer. I tried to decipher it at Langley and realized too late that the file had a worm that warned the Ghost Squad of a leak, and where. The rest, as they say, is history."

Abby nodded. "Where does that leave us? Who can we trust?"

Ben frowned. "Good question. Fred, I presume you had your reasons for playing dead."

"You've got that right. Two of the names on the memo's pass-around list are my superiors. In fact, the list is a Who's Who of muckety mucks. Not just those in the government, but in major corporations, media conglomerates, you name it."

"I guess that means the press is out, too," Abby murmured.

"How about Barksdale?" Ben asked. "Did he get the memo, too?"

"I was pleasantly surprised to see that it specifically spelled out the dire consequences to be had, should he learn of Flamingo."

Suddenly Ben leaped up. "I know who should deliver the message." He grabbed Abby's hand and pulled her out of the booth with him. "We have to hurry, before it's too late!"

"Who?" Fred asked, as he stuffed a couple of twenties in the waitress's hand.

"Supreme Court Justice Roberta Gordon. But we have to act fast. Today she is submitting her resignation to the president."

CHAPTER 55

Fred's kamikaze driving got them down Sixteenth Street without a police escort. "What are we supposed to do, just waltz right in without an invitation?" he asked.

"I was one of Barksdale's largest donors. The First Lady, Sarah, is quite aware of this."

"Abby, I hate to remind you, but the First Lady just attended your funeral. Despite your reputation for sainthood, I doubt seriously she'll take a call from you."

Abby smiled. "She'll take one from Maddy. Especially when Maddy reminds her that Abby underwrote the restoration of the Roosevelt Room's oil painting of Teddy, during his Rough Rider stage. She knows Abby was to have picked it up this week. I'll tell her that I'll be there in her stead, with the restorer and his aide, so that he can complete the work before he is due to return to the Louvre next month."

"Brilliant." Ben breathed a sigh of relief. "Once we're inside, we'll be steps away from the Oval Office, where President Barksdale is to accept Roberta's resignation."

Fred let them out on Pennsylvania Avenue, a block from the White House's East Executive Avenue guard station. The undulating crowd—which consisted of tourists, government workers, and the always ubiquitous protesters—soon closed around them.

The two-man White House security detail was wary when Abby approached them, but her knowledge of the First Lady's direct line convinced them that she might indeed be someone who Sarah Barksdale was expecting.

Their escort arrived in a golf cart. The journey from there to the West Wing was the longest of Ben's life.

It was Justice Roberta Gordon's opinion that Benjamin Brinker was a sight for sore eyes, no matter where she should find him.

Not that she expected him to be dashing down the hall toward her, just as Vice President Talbot was escorting her into the Oval Office.

Hearing Ben call out her name, she turned around—

As did Talbot.

She watched as Talbot's eyes narrowed; how he gave a slight nod to the Secret Service agent closest to him.

She turned toward Ben. Despite his congenial smile and declaration to Talbot's security detail that they should have "No worries! The Supreme Court Justice and I are old friends..." the look in his eye was one she'd seen before—when he was younger, and determined to be the champion who could right all wrongs. It was the look he had when he was excited about the candidates he felt—no, he *knew*—could make the world a better place.

She had been worried about his silence these past few days, since the horrible crash that took Andy and sweet Abigail's lives. Whatever Ben was up to, she knew it was important, and that she had to help him succeed.

Talbot's Secret Service agent tried to block her old friend from reaching her, but Ben's underhanded toss sent something tiny—a

USB flash drive, from the look of it, with some comic book character drawn on it—hurtling her way.

The urgency of Ben's words—*"Make sure Barksdale sees this, no matter what"*—intrigued her, as did the fact that Talbot was more angry than surprised about the chain of events.

The flash drive dropped and skittered to a halt right in front of her.

So when Talbot reached down for it, Roberta thought nothing at all about pressing her heel on his hand.

When he jerked it away, she grabbed it first. "I think this was meant for me," she purred sweetly.

Before he could respond, she strolled into the Oval Office, shutting the door behind her.

Roberta was determined that Ben's detention with his Secret Service interrogators be short and sweet: perhaps no longer than her meeting with President Barksdale.

She didn't resign, as intended and expected. Instead, she insisted the thumb drive was a gift to the president—

One which he should open right then and there, in her presence.

Her calm but steely tone encouraged him to oblige her.

She read over his shoulder as he opened one file after another on something called Operation Flamingo.

Should it succeed, thousands of Americans would lose their lives. Political factions would rally a frightened constituency to insist he declare war on a country that had nothing to do with the tragedy. And to Barksdale's horror, his second-in-command, a man he despised, would use the incident to catapult himself into the presidency.

He sat silently, numbed by the evidence confronting him.

"You must arrest the vice president immediately," Roberta reasoned with him.

"But Roberta...I—"

She waved his hesitation away with an elegant hand. "He is committing treason, and framing innocent men for his crimes. And he has murdered his political opponent. It could just as easily have been you, Mr. President. After all, only you now stand in his way."

Barksdale blanched at that thought, until she added, "Edward, you must protect your presidential legacy. Otherwise you too will be implicated, and you too will face impeachment and criminal proceedings, for high crimes, based on this evidence."

Barksdale sighed. She was right. The last thing he'd want his enemies to chant was: "What did Barksdale know, and when did he know it?"

He buzzed for his chief of security.

When the man came, Roberta sat silently as the president growled, "Arrest the vice president."

"Oh, and Mr. President? The young man who uncovered the scheme must be released immediately from Secret Service custody. I suggest he be brought here to you, so that he may fill you in on all he knows."

CHAPTER 56

By the time Ben, Abby and Fred had been debriefed, there were less than five hours to go before the Pacific Time countdown to midnight.

Talbot was denying everything. He pleaded the fifth, and asked to see his lawyer.

Talbot was put in lockdown, but his staff and family were told that he had joined the president at Camp David. His cell phones and computers, both at his office in the Eisenhower building and in his official residence—Number One Observatory Circle, on the grounds of the United States Naval Observatory—had been confiscated, and were being searched for any incriminating evidence.

Fail-safe for Operation Flamingo was to be confirmed via text from Smith to Talbot, from a cell phone listed under the name of Talbot's six-year-old grandson.

Smith would text: *Grandpa, thanks for taking me to the movies this weekend!*

The mission would be aborted if Talbot texted back, *Sorry, Jimmy, I've got to work.*

Talbot never texted back.

Because he didn't trust Talbot, Smith texted his mole inside the veep's office to ask about his boss's whereabouts. The response—*with POTUS, at Camp David with families*—made him breathe easier.

All systems were go.

He signaled the ranch operatives to load the human bombs into the vans, then he hopped into the one holding Digits. He would personally place the kid in the middle of a crowd in the center of the Las Vegas Strip. That way, he'd be certain that this would be Digits' last night on Earth.

StratCom was in a bit of a quandary. If Special Ops swooped down in helicopters with bullhorns to warn the gathered crowds, pandemonium would ensue on the Vegas Strip, perhaps even a stampede.

And even if the crowd dispersed to hide in their hotel rooms, the bombers might actually go inside with them, making it even harder for Spec Ops to track them down before the bombs went off.

The president shook his head. "We've got to disarm the bombs quietly and covertly. Is that possible?"

General Pendergrass, StratCom's senior commander, nodded. "Three of the hotels have rooftop helipads. We're flying through secured military airspace, so we can be on the ground in four hours, tops. Since the human bombs are drugged and unwilling, the terrorists are using a radio frequency to detonate the bombs. Spec Ops will get as close as possible to the human bombs. They'll have jammers that will block the signal. The ops team will be wearing plain clothes. They also have fake cameras equipped with face recognition technology, to seek out the human bombs. But there's a problem: from what Mr. Brinker tells us, the teenager,

Digits, is the only human bomb who was not pictured in the dossier. In fact, because of his covert nature and the fact that he is an illegal alien, no pictures of him exist."

"Both Fred and I would know him, even if he were disguised," Ben declared.

"I take it you won't mind coming along then?" the general asked.

Ben shook his head. "I insist."

It was the least he could do for Andy.

It was all that was left to do for Maddy.

"Promise you'll come back to me," were Abby's last words to Ben.

He didn't need any encouragement to stay alive. Still, her gentle kiss was icing on the cake.

It kept him from considering the consequences, should he fail to recognize Digits.

No, failure was not an option.

CHAPTER 57

Ben walked through the wall-to-wall humanity that cheered and shrieked and laughed in front of the Bellagio. Through his earpiece, he heard the Ops commander mutter, "God almighty, it's like looking for a needle in a haystack. We're at zero minus eight minutes, Green Team."

He circled the man-made lake in front of the deluxe hotel, scanning every face as he walked through the crowd. Periodically, he'd hear a whoop in his earpiece as various other teams—Pink, for the one at the Flamingo; Blue, for the team monitoring the MGM Grand; Yellow, for Circus Circus; Brown, for Treasure Island; Purple, for the Venetian; and Orange, for the Stratosphere—identified their suspects, and ferried them out of the crowd, so that the process of disarming them could be done in the privacy of a van.

Still no Digits.

"Just two minutes to go, Green Team," the mission commander warned.

Ben tried to stick to type: short, thin males. More than likely, Digits would be standing alone, despite a proximity to others. He wouldn't be moving, despite the activity around him.

And he wouldn't be talking. Ben had no trouble remembering his own reaction to the drugs Smith had injected in him—

Smith.

There was Smith, right in front of him.

With Digits.

Granted, the younger man's hair was cropped shorter. He wore rounded glasses, and his hair was tipped blond. Still, it was Digits, alright.

"Sighted Digits—and *Smith*," he fairly shouted.

The bomb expert he was teamed with ran over. "Let's go! Quick!"

They dove into the crowd, which was now counting down the seconds:

46...45...44...43...42...

Ben pushed his way through it—

"There he is!" Ben cried out. "Blue jacket, with argyle vest!"

As the bomb pro yanked the jacket off Digits and went to work, Ben rushed through the crowd.

Where was Smith?

Was that it? Was he going to disappear into the crowd, just walk away?

Over Ben's dead body.

It was Smith who assassinated his friend, Andy.

And it was Smith who had murdered beautiful sad bittersweet Maddy.

No, Smith wasn't going to get away. Not this time.

Yes there he was...

As if sensing Ben coming, Smith turned around—but it was too late.

With all his might Ben leaped through the air, landing on Smith's chest.

He was prepared for Smith's dirty punches. But he wasn't prepared for the gun pulled from his back. He held it out and aimed it at Ben—

Only to get it knocked out of his hand by three very drunk women, who were whooping for joy at the hotel's fireworks.

Both Ben and Smith scrambled on their hands and knees through the legs of the revelers.

It was Ben who came up holding it. Smith held out his hand as if it were a pistol, as if mocking him:

Bang bang, you're dead.

He knows I'll never shoot a gun in this mob, Ben thought, as he watched the man duck through the crowd, and saunter into the hotel—

No way in hell is he going to get away.

Ben sprinted into the hotel. The lobby was packed, but the revelers, hoping to catch the Bellagio's signature fireworks before they ended, were streaming out of the casino, in the opposite direction.

Ben ran to the elevator banks. If Smith had caught one, he could be hiding out on any of the hotel's thirty-six floors. He was just about to give up when it came to him—

The Bellagio's botanical gardens.

He ran down the hall toward the garden room.

The sign on the door proclaiming that the gardens were closed, was swaying, if only slightly.

Smith was in there.

Ben opened the door slowly.

The garden was decked out for the holidays. The paths on the floor were lined with a sea of bright red poinsettias. Beautifully decorated Christmas trees flanked the walls. Three feet tall snowflakes hung from the ceiling. Six man-sized gingerbread houses fronted a Christmas tree tall enough to reach the stained glass atrium in the middle of the room.

So, where was Smith?

Ben raised his gun, only to have his arm kicked by Smith,

causing Ben to fire skyward.

The bullet hit the glass ceiling.

Ben barely had time to duck into one of the gingerbread houses before a shower of glass shards fell on them.

Smith screamed as a jagged pane of glass pierced his leg.

Ben ran after Smith as he stumbled out the door.

His trail of blood led to the casino. Ben dodged in and out of the rows of one-armed bandits and the gamblers who sat in front of them. At first he didn't see Smith. Then someone hit a jackpot.

All heads turned toward the bells and whistles. That's when he saw Smith, dodging out a side exit.

When Ben opened it, he found himself back out in front of the Bellagio's fountain.

He walked slowly to the left, glancing at all the faces he passed. Everyone was still and looking skyward at the fireworks.

But one man was limping toward the street.

When Smith looked back, Ben took a girl in his arms and kissed her. Over her shoulder, he noticed Smith smiling, satisfied he had lost Ben. The injured man slowed his gait. He even decided to take in some of the fireworks.

That was his big mistake.

Ben's tackle threw them both into the hotel's large, shallow pool. Smith tried to claw his way out of Ben's chokehold that held him underwater for what seemed like an eternity, but Ben was too strong for him.

The light show above them illuminated Smith's face through the water.

Ben enjoyed watching the fear in Smith's eyes as the drowning man realized he wasn't really a ghost after all.

It was Fred who finally pulled Ben away from Smith's limp body.

CHAPTER 58

Talbot finally folded when he was told that the terrorist attack had been stopped, and that a rogue black ops asset named John Smith had been arrested at the scene. Besides verifying the names of the other DC power brokers in league with him, he insisted that Smith was the mastermind of the scheme; that the spook even went so far as to providing Talbot with false intel in order to justify the attack, despite its illegality, and the deaths that would be incurred.

Talbot's formal defense plea actually stated: "However misguided, when it came to his love of his country and its people, it was the vice president's conviction that the needs of the many outweighed the needs of the few."

It was the defense's hope that there might actually be enough *Star Trek* fans on the grand jury to save his ass.

Talbot reasoned that when the others were also faced with indictments, they too would spill their guts. And like he, they'd follow through on their pact to make Smith the fall guy.

Maybe they'd get lucky and the SWAT team would take Smith out. For all their sakes, he hoped so.

On the flight home, it was confirmed that all the human

bombs had been located and defused in time, without the New Year's Eve crowd's knowledge.

It was also confirmed that Smith had been resuscitated in the ambulance that took him away.

And that he had escaped after killing the EMT who revived him.

Ben frowned. "I guess I'll always be looking over my shoulder for that ghoul," he said to Fred.

Fred shook his head. "Nah. Spooks don't hold grudges. It's just business."

Ben didn't believe him. At this point, he found it hard to believe anyone who made his living inside the 202 Area Code.

He couldn't wait to get home to Abby and tell her he loved her.

He wondered if she'd believe him. One way or another, he'd prove that was the case.

EIGHT MONTHS LATER

"Hand me those hedge clippers, will you Benjamin?" Roberta asked, as she wiped the sweat off her brow.

Ben gladly obliged. He'd been on his knees in that flowerbed all morning. Any excuse to stretch his legs worked for him.

As he handed them to her, he warned, "Don't trim that hedge too low. Abby likes her privacy."

Roberta guffawed. "I'd say she's got nothing to worry about. Alquith Hall is the middle of nowhere."

"That's fine by us," Abby piped up from her Adirondack chair. "We like life in the slow lane."

Roberta laughed. "In your condition, I guess you would. How far along are you now?"

"Four months and six days," Ben said, as he patted Abby's rounded belly.

Their guest smiled. "Have you thought about names?"

Ben and Abby exchanged glances. "Andrew and Maddy," Abby murmured.

Roberta sighed. "I see. Then for your sake, I hope it's a girl."

It was Ben's turn to laugh. "Oh it is, Roberta. *And* a boy. Twins."

Roberta stopped mid-clip. "Well, you'll certainly have your hands full! No wonder you turned down Ferguson's request to handle his senatorial campaign."

"Nope, I turned him down, because of his voting record." Ben shrugged. "Not to mention his finance sources."

"You're right. He doesn't deserve you. Then again, according to the latest poll, he may not have needed you after all. Seems that all the Democrats are having a cakewalk this time around."

"With the GOP's presidential frontrunner in prison, and so many of their backers indicted, I guess it was inevitable." Ben smiled.

"Abby, how's Lavinia doing these days?" Roberta's clippers stopped for a moment, so that she could look back and assess her handiwork.

"Just fine, I guess. We so rarely see her. She's so used to the city now, it's almost impossible to convince her to spend any time out here with us."

"I sent flowers to the house, after Preston's death. I got back the sweetest note from her."

"She truly appreciated them. She didn't get many," Abby explained. After his indictment, she found out pretty quickly who her real friends are."

"Well, you know what they say. If you want a true friend in Washington, get a dog." Ben speared the ground with a hoe.

"Frankly, I think Preston got off easy," Abby murmured. "His fatal heart attack couldn't have been timed more perfectly: just a few days after his indictment."

"Abby's got her own conspiracy theory," Ben explained. "She thinks he made a pact with Smith to kill him before he went to trial, and now Smith is off on some tropical island with his blood money. Frankly, I can believe it."

Roberta shuddered. "I hope she's right. I'd much rather have that killer a million miles from here." She patted Abby's hand. "I'm also happy you don't have to testify."

Abby nodded. "Me too. I guess we were lucky that the files on the digital dossier provided enough evidence to convict the traitors."

"That, and all the video feeds of Talbot plotting and scheming in his limo with some shadowy figure," Ben added. "It was sent in from some anonymous source. My guess is that both are the same man: Mr. Smith."

"I'm too smart to take that bet," Roberta laughed. "Tell me, Abby, does anyone even suspect you aren't really Maddy?"

Abby shook her head. "No. And that's fine by me. Maddy may have had many things wrong, but she had one thing right: you don't need to live in the spotlight to be happy."

Ben laughed. "Oh yeah? Then what do you need?"

"That's easy. All you need is a man who proves his love for you, every day."

Ben scooped his wife into his arms and held her tight.

That may have been enough for him, but not for her. She cupped her palm behind his neck and drew his mouth to hers. Her lips grazed his, for one tantalizing minute, before the kiss deepened into the bliss he ached for whenever she was within view.

Eventually he drew back, but his eyes didn't want to leave her. Instead, they took in everything he loved about his wife. Her open laugh. Her broad, welcoming smile. Her steady, adoring gaze from those deep blue eyes.

Even with her hair still dyed Maddy's dark auburn, whenever he looked at her, Maddy's ghost never stared back at him.

He now realized she has all the traits he had sought but had found missing in her emotionally bereft sister.

Appreciation. Respect. Trust.

Love.

And when in love, as she once was with Andy, as she was now

with Ben, Abby was capable of doing anything.

Even saving the world.

Even saving Ben.

OTHER NOVELS BY JOSIE BROWN

THE HOUSEWIFE ASSASSIN SERIES

The Housewife Assassin's Handbook
(Book 1)

The Housewife Assassin's Guide to Gracious Killing
(Book 2)

The Housewife Assassin's Killer Christmas Tips
(Book 3)

The Housewife Assassin's Relationship Survival Guide
(Book 4)

The Housewife Assassin's Vacation to Die For
(Book 5)

The Housewife Assassin's Recipes for Disaster
(Book 6)

The Housewife Assassin's Hollywood Scream Play
(Book 7)

The Housewife Assassin's Deadly Dossier
(The Series Prequel)

The Housewife Assassin's Killer App
(Book 8)

The Housewife Assassin's Hostage Hosting Tips
(Book 9)

The Housewife Assassin's Garden of Deadly Delights
(Book 10)

*The Housewife Assassin's Tips for
Weddings, Weapons, and Warfare*
(Book 11)

The Housewife Assassin's Husband Hunting Hints
(Book 12)

The Housewife Assassin's Ghost Protocol
(Book 13)

The Housewife Assassin's Terrorist TV Guide
(Book 14)

THE TRUE HOLLYWOOD LIES SERIES

Hollywood Hunk

Hollywood Whore

THE TOTLANDIA SERIES

The Onesies - Book 1 (Fall)

The Onesies - Book 2 (Winter)

The Onesies - Book 3 (Spring)

The Onesies - Book 4 (Summer)

The Twosies - Book 5 (Fall)

The Twosies - Book 6 (Winter)

MORE JOSIE BROWN NOVELS

The Candidate

Secret Lives of Husbands and Wives

The Baby Planner

Made in the USA
San Bernardino, CA
30 March 2017